M000028104

Take Back The Streets!

"Let's hit it, Mojo," Wolff barked to his co-pilot/systems operator, as he dropped the nose of his Tactical Police Griffin chopper out of the night sky. "This is Zero One, form up on me. We'll come in from the north, and run a race track until Tac One can gain cover. Then we'll do a little close up air support work on these maggots. How copy?"

The other three TPF gunships radioed their acknowledgment as they got into formation.

"Tac One, this is Dragon One Zero. Any time you're ready."

"Tac One, copy. Now!"

The choppers swooped down on cue. When they were within 500 meters of the small apartment building-turned-gang-stronghold, Mojo pressed the trigger. The Griffin's airframe shuddered under the recoil of the heavy 25mm HE shells as he walked his fire from right to left, sweeping the line of the top story windows.

Huge chunks of brick and concrete fell to the empty streets below. There was scattered return fire from the lower floors, but nothing heavy. Mojo kept up a steady stream till Wolff banked away over the building to clear the line of fire for the next ship.

"Zero One to Zero Two. You're on, Gunner. Make it count!"

THE EXECUTIONER
by Don Pendleton

Available wherever paperbacks are sold, or order direct from the Publisher. Send cover price plus 50¢ per copy for mailing and handling to Pinnacle Books, Dept. 17-353, 475 Park Avenue South, New York, N.Y. 10016. Residents of New York, New Jersey and Pennsylvania must include sales tax. DO NOT SEND CASH.

CHOPPER COPS
RICK MACKIN

PINNACLE BOOKS
WINDSOR PUBLISHING CORP.

To
The men and women of the Springfield, Oregon Police Department

PINNACLE BOOKS

are published by

Windsor Publishing Corp.
475 Park Avenue South
New York, NY 10016

Copyright © 1990 by Michael Wm. Kasner

All rights reserved. No part of this book may be repro-
duced in any form or by any means without the prior
written consent of the Publisher, excepting brief quotes
used in reviews.

First printing: May, 1990

Printed in the United States of America

CHAPTER 1

Seattle, Washington. September 1999

Five thousand feet above The Puget Sound, a dull black, shark-like helicopter cruised through the moonless night sky. The chopper flew with no navigation lights and the sound of its rotors could not be heard from the water. Had it been daylight, yellow letters reading U.S.T.P.F. would have been visible on the sides and belly of the machine identifying it as belonging to the United States Tactical Police Force.

This was a new shape in the skies over Seattle, a Bell Model 506P Griffin police helicopter, the hottest rotary wing machine ever to fly. And the men flying it were the elite of the most elite police force in the world, the chopper cops of the United States Tactical Police Force Dragon Flight.

In the armored cockpit of the Griffin, the dull red night flying lights from the instrument panel illuminated two men in dark police blue flight helmets and coveralls with a colorful patch over the right breast pocket depicting a winged dragon. The man in the right pilot's seat flew the sleek machine with delicate, practiced movements while the co-pilot/systems operator in the left seat watched the sensor instruments on the console to his left. The co-pilot, a black man with a shaved head and a bushy mustache, shook his head and keyed his throat mike.

"Sorry 'bout that, Wolfman," Tactical Police Flight Officer Jumal "Mojo" Mugabe told the pilot over the intercom. "Still nothing."

5

Federal Tactical Police Force Flight Sergeant Rick "Wolfman" Wolff, grinned slowly under his face shield. Wolff was tall, easy going and good looking. "No sweat, Mojo," he answered. "I don't mind flying around on a beautiful summer night like this, do you?"

Mugabe looked up from his sensors for a quick glance through the canopy. To their left, the sparkling lights of the sprawling metropolis of Greater Seattle spread for miles along the sound. In the late summer of 1999, Seattle was the new financial and cultural center of the west coast of the United States and dominated the ever-growing Pacific Rim trade. In less than a decade, the city had grown from a mere 750 thousand citizens to a staggering three million. With this unparalleled growth, however, had come severe problems.

Crime always follows money and, as Seattle had grown, criminal gangs had swarmed to the city like vultures to a fat calf. Once established in the sprawling metropolis, they battled among themselves for a bigger piece of the vice and crime industry. The TPF's mission tonight was to interdict a boatload of stolen Army weapons before even more blood was spilled on the streets of Seattle.

None of this violence was apparent from the air, however. All that could be seen were the sparkling lights and highrise buildings crowding the waterfront. From the air, Greater Seattle was a beautiful sight.

"This is a great night for it," Mugabe agreed before looking back down again. "How about making one more pass?"

"Roger that," Wolff said. Pushing down on the rudder pedal and shoving the cyclic control over against the stop, he banked the sleek, dull black Griffin over on her side and snapped her tail around for another flight over the sound.

For the last decade, police departments all over the country had employed helicopters on an ever increasing basis. But there were drawbacks to the police flying choppers that had been originally designed for civilian use. They were expensive to operate and there was limited space in the airframes to accommodate radio and electronic equipment. In the late 1990's, however, a spectacular new machine had come on the scene that met the specific needs of police work, specifically tactical police work.

When the "Cold War" died in the early 1990s much of the nation's military high technology was turned to police applications. While this infusion of technology gave police quite a bit of sophisticated new equipment, the best result was the new specialized police helicopter, the Bell Model 506P Griffin. While its lineage went back to the Bell AH-1 Cobra of the Vietnam War, this was the first helicopter designed from the ground up specifically for police use.

Designed with low maintenance costs in mind, the Griffin was powered by two small, but powerful, 750 shaft horsepower General Electric turbines pod mounted externally on the fuselage, driving a four bladed rigid rotor with a diameter of only 40 feet. Both the main rotor and the shrouded tail rotor had been designed for noise suppression as well as maximum maneuverability. Not only was the Griffin quick and stable, it was quiet.

With a crew of two, pilot and co-pilot/systems operator, the Griffin could carry up to six people or 1,500 pounds of cargo in the rear compartment. An electric winch controlled from the cockpit allowed for the movement of equipment or personnel to and from the rear compartment.

Protective measures built into the Griffin included: backup flight controls, self-sealing fuel tanks, armored nacelles for the turbines, an armored crew compartment with a bullet-proof Lexan canopy and Kevlar seats. In normal circumstances, the Griffin was immune to ground fire up to and including 7.62mm armor-piercing ammunition.

The heart of the Griffin, however, were in its sensors and communications systems that had been borrowed directly from the military. Using either the active infrared or light intensifying system, the Griffin could see in the dark under almost any conditions. Working in conjunction with a terrain following radar navigation and mapping system, this allowed the pilot to know where he was at all times, day or night. All of the sensors were tied into the aircrew's helmets and digital readouts and could be seen either on the helmet visor or on a HUD, heads up display, in the cockpit. Digital data link capability allowed both computer and sensor data to be sent between the Griffin and ground stations.

While not primarily a gunship, the Griffin was capable of being armed with a variety of weapons in its nose turret and on the stub wing weapon's pylons. A 40mm grenade launcher was fitted to the 360-degree turret that could select from a variety of ordnance to include flash-bang grenades, tear gas bombs, smoke cartridges, or a low fragmentation HE round. Also, a select fire, 7.62mm Chain gun was mounted beside the grenade launcher. All of the weapons systems were controlled by the co-pilot/systems operator, but could be fired by the pilot if necessary. As with the sensors, the weapons were slaved to the helmets with the visor serving as the weapons sight as well as providing weapons status data.

Not only was the Griffin a completely different kind of police helicopter, the TPF Dragon Flight officers who flew the Griffins were a new breed of police officer, the elite troops of the elite of federal law enforcement. With the drastic cutback in American military forces in the '90s, men who would have become hot-rock fighter jocks were instead now flying Griffins for the TPF. These were the "Top Guns" of the '90s. Young, quick and fearless, they saw themselves as the nation's first line of defense in the war against the powerful criminal elements who threatened to take over the country.

The Dragon Flight was a highly mobile tactical police unit which could speed to anywhere in the country at a moment's notice. Within hours of a call, the four Griffin helicopters, a twenty-man Tactical Platoon, a headquarters staff and their support troops could be on the ground and in the air fighting any crime emergency that was too big for the local authorities to handle. Tonight was one of those times and the two Tac Force cops were putting it on the line again.

"I think I've got him!" Mugabe shouted. "Bearing one-five-four range four thousand meters, headed for shore right above the point. He's got his running lights off and going like a bat outa hell. He's doing at least fifty knots and

8

leaving a beautiful IR trace. It's got to be a hovercraft."

Wolff keyed his throat mike and relayed the message to TPF Lieutenant Jack Zumwald, the commander of the Tactical Platoon, and his mobile unit on the shore, vectoring them in to intercept the hovercraft at what appeared would be its destination, a darkened and deserted dock and warehouse site at the end of the industrial area.

"Zoomie says thanks," Wolff passed the message from the Tac Platoon officer.

Mugabe patted the top of instrument panel that fed him information from the chopper's high tech sensors. "Piece of cake with this baby."

Now that the hovercraft had been spotted, Wolff flew his Griffin a little farther out over the water, away from his target. He knew that with the Griffin's computered-controlled chameleon "mirror skin" set to matte black, whoever was on the boat couldn't see them on a moonless night. But he didn't want to take a chance that they might hear the suppressed beat of their rotors. Sound did strange things over water. The pilot selected the targeting visual readout on his HUD, Head Up Display, on the inside of the canopy and watched the hovercraft cut its speed and make for the darkened dock.

Suddenly, TPF ground support searchlights burst into life from the dockside, pinpointing the boat. In the glare of the lights, Wolff saw a man step out with a loudspeaker in his hands. The gunrunners didn't even give him a chance to order them to surrender, they immediately opened up with a storm of automatic weapons fire, shattering the lights.

"Let's get him!" Wolff shouted, throwing the Griffin into a dive. Twisting the throttle all the way against the stop, he squeezed the radio switch on the collective control. "Control, this is One Zero," he transmitted. "Suspect vessel opened fire on the mobile unit and we're going after him."

"Control, copy," came the reply in his headphones. "Keep on him, don't let him get away."

"One Zero, copy. He's not going anywhere tonight."

Wolff toggled the switch to the retracted SX-18 Nightsun searchlights in the belly of the Griffin. The powerful, million candlepower beams dropped down from their housings and lit up the fleeing hovercraft. A second switch activated the loudspeaker system. "This is the Tactical Police Force," he announced. "Stop your boat!"

Wolff's message was answered by a burst of automatic weapons fire. The pilot switched off the lights as he threw the Griffin out of the way of the stream of dull red tracers. There was no sense in giving them an aiming point.

"Control, this is One Zero," he radioed back to the TPF TOC, the Tactical Operations Center. "We're taking fire."

"Control copy, Rules of Engagement Charlie are in effect," the TOC radioed back. This ROE gave him permission to blow the gunrunners out of the water without giving them a second chance.

"One Zero X-ray, copy," Mugabe answered as he flicked the switch to the 40mm grenade launcher and the 7.62mm Chain gun in the Griffin's nose turret. Time to go to work. He dialed the high explosive ammunition feed for the 40mm and armor-piercing tracer rounds for the Chain gun as he centered the speeding hovercraft in the weapons sight displayed on his helmet visor.

Unlike the earlier electric motor driven, multi-barrel Vulcans and Mini-guns, the Chain gun was a single barrel weapon that could be fired at a variable rate ranging from a single shot to 900 rounds per minute. The rate of fire was controlled by the gunner's trigger. A light touch fired a single shot, but laying back on the trigger unleashed the full power of the weapon. This time, Mugabe wasn't holding anything back.

His gloved fingers tightened around the firing controls, his right hand controlling the Chain gun and the left hand the 40 mike. The Griffin shuddered as Mugabe opened up. A stream of red tracer fire raced down to meet the bow of the hovercraft.

Not only was the Chain gun fast, it was accurate. The turret's gun aiming system automatically compensated for recoil, re-aiming the gun ten times a second while it was firing. As long as Mugabe had the target locked in his gunsight, he would hit it. And hit it he did.

10

7.62mm armor-piercing rounds chewed into the boat. Pieces of metal and wood flew into the air. As Wolff bored in closer, Mugabe walked his line of fire back toward the bridge of the boat. Although Rules of Engagement Charlie allowed him to use maximum force, he wanted to try to stop the boat without sinking it or killing all of the crew.

Suddenly, a stream of bright red tracer fire leapt up at the TPF chopper, heavy machinegun fire. Wolff dumped his collective and stomped down on the rudder pedal to throw his machine out of the line of fire. The blacked out ship skidded in the air, but not before the Griffin took several hits along her nose. Sparks flew as the bullets bounced off the armored skin and bulletproof Lexan plastic canopy.

"You hit?" Wolff asked as he hauled the chopper around and lined up on the target again.

"He took out the IR sensor head," Mugabe said grimly. "But everything else seems to be working."

"Time we quit fucking around with this asshole," Wolff growled. "Zero his ass now!"

"You got it."

Sighting in on the huge ducted fans at the rear of the hovercraft, Mugabe squeezed off a six-round burst from the grenade launcher. One of the 40 mm HE grenades punched through the thin metal of a fuel tank before detonating. The explosion engulfed the speeding hovercraft in a boiling fireball. In the glare of the fire, Wolff would see men with their clothes on fire leaping into The Puget Sound. The boat slowed and settled in the water. In seconds, it was all over.

"Control, this is One Zero," he radioed. "Suspect boat is neutralized and dead in the water."

"Control copy, the Tac Platoon will clean up after you. Return to base."

"One Zero, copy."

Wolff took one last look at the burning hulk in the water. When were these scumbags ever going to learn not to screw around with Tac Force Griffin choppers? Flicking his navigation lights on, he gently banked the helicopter around and headed for the Coast Guard Station the Tac Force was using as a temporary base during their stay in Seattle.

* * *

It was a short flight back to the Coast Guard Station at the western end of Seattle and when Wolff and Mugabe stepped out of their ship, they found their commander, TPF Captain J.D. "Buzz" Corcran, waiting for them outside the Tactical Operations Center van. An older, balding, barrel-chested man, Corcran had had a long career flying military and police helicopters before he had become the commander of the first TPF Dragon Flight. Even though he was stuck behind a commander's desk, he still considered himself a gunship pilot first. And at times like this, he secretly envied the two flyers walking toward him. They had fought the battle, while all he could do was sit and listen to it over the radio.

"I just got a call from Zumwald," Corcran greeted them. "There were illegal weapons on board that boat, but they were just a bunch of Red Chinese made AK-94s," the captain sounded disgusted. "And a couple of RPG-9s."

The Red Chinese AK-94 5.56mm assault rifle and 88mm RPG-9 anti-tank rocket launcher were definitely bad news in the wrong hands, but they weren't nearly as dangerous as the weapons they had hoped to find. A week earlier, a shipment of the latest high tech U.S. Army weapons had been hijacked from a convoy traveling from Fort Lewis. The shipment had included the assault rifles, anti-tank rockets, and anti-aircraft missiles. The Dragon Flight had been dispatched from their home base in Denver to get those weapons back in the right hands ASAP.

"Shit!" Wolff said. "I was sure we had 'em."

"It looks like our information was off again." The TPF captain turned to go back into the TOC. "You two hot shots better get some sleep tonight. I've got you scheduled for ramp alert in the morning."

"Captain," Wolff spoke up. "I'd like Red to look over our ship first. We took some hits tonight."

"You'd better get him going on it then," Corcran said. "I want all four choppers up and ready to go first thing in the morning."

"Yes sir."

"That sure as hell takes care of our plans for the evening," Wolff said.

"Guess we'll just have to wait till tomorrow to see the delights of this jewel of the Northwest," Mugabe shrugged.

"That's the thrilling life of a chopper cop in the TPF," Wolff said.

"Right."

CHAPTER 2

Snoqualmie National Forest.

Winston J. Patterson III, looked down the railroad track that ran through the cut in the towering fir trees on the side of the mountain. The two-engine train was just starting its run up the long grade to the top of the pass. The old Vietnamese, Nguyen Cao Dong, had been right after all; the train carrying the nuclear missiles was right on time.

He turned around to look at the six people he had brought with him, four young men and two women. They were bent over the track a hundred meters uphill from him unbolting a section of the rail. "Hurry up!" he shouted. "It's coming!"

While the others finished dragging the length of rail track off to the side and dropped it, Patterson quickly arranged the railroad signal devices on the track in the "Danger, Stop Immediately" pattern. When the engineer spotted the signals, he would automatically slam on the brakes. The train was going slowly enough that it should have time to stop, but he really didn't care if it did hit the place where the track was missing and derailed. All he cared about was stopping it, one way or the other.

When Dong had first come to him with information about the train, Patterson had been suspicious. As the founder and self-appointed leader of the Mother Earth Liberation Army, he would have welcomed that kind of intelligence from any of the other environmental freedom fighters, but Dong was Vietnamese. He'd had a difficult time understanding why an Asian wanted to get involved in the residents' struggle to keep the Northwest free from nuclear weapons. The only Asians he had ever met were the most dedicated capitalists in the world and capitalists were generally not noted for their concern about the environment.

But after Dong had made a very sizeable financial contribution to Patterson's organization, the environmental terrorist had been convinced that he was sincere and welcomed him into the inner circle of the M.E.L.A.

Then Dong had brought him the information about the next "White Train" shipment of Trident II missiles and a plan to keep them from being delivered to the Navy's submarine base at Bangor. The trains weren't painted white, of course; the government had stopped marking them that way a long time ago. Nowadays the Nuclear Weapons Commission tried to sneak the missiles into the base on trains disguised as regular freight haulers, but the name was still used.

Patterson had to admit that Dong's plan was ingenious. When he had first learned of the train, Patterson had wanted to stop it when it reached Greater Seattle and hold it hostage until the government agreed to remove the missiles. That was the only way he knew how to get the media exposure that he so desperately needed. Television coverage of a nuclear weapons train being held hostage in the city would awaken the masses to the danger of these weapons. But when he had outlined his idea to Dong, the Vietnamese had accurately pointed out that those tactics had not been very successful in the past. In an urban area, it was too easy for the police to break up the planned demonstration with riot gas before anyone had even learned that it was happening.

Instead, Dong had suggested that they stop the train in the mountain pass, disable it and then notify the press. That way, not only would it be very difficult for the authorities to retrieve the cargo of missiles, the environmentalists wouldn't have to run the risk of a bloody confrontation with the police. Patterson had liked that part of the plan best. He wanted to be known as the man who had made the Northwest safe for the people, but he didn't want to get his head busted while he was doing it.

He placed the last signal on the track and ran up to where the others waited back in the treeline. Xuan, the Vietnamese observer that Dong had sent, was waiting there as well. Dong had said that he couldn't come himself to see how well the plan worked, but he had sent one of his aides, a sinister, hatchet-faced man, along as an observer. Patterson hadn't liked the idea of having a stranger around, but since Dong had planned the operation, he had consented.

The booming sound of the first explosive signal echoed through the trees. By the time the second one went off, sparks showered the tracks from the steel driving wheels of the powerful diesel locomotives as the engineer locked his brakes. The train had no sooner ground to a shuddering halt when a squad of men in camouflage uniforms and red berets rushed from the treeline for the train. When the engineer looked out his window and saw them, he reached for the button to sound the alarm. One of the attackers fired a long burst from his U.S. Army M-25 assault rifle through the open window and blew the man in half. The assault squad raced for the Army MP security detachment riding in the caboose.

The stunned soldiers were overcome almost before they could lock and load their weapons. Their officer, a young MP lieutenant, was cut down by a grenade thrown through the door. He never even had a chance to radio a message for help.

Patterson couldn't believe what he was seeing. "My God!" he shouted spinning around to face Xuan. "Who are those men!"

"They are the Boa Hoa," the Vietnamese said over the roar of the small arms fire. "They work for Colonel Dong."

"What are you doing?" Patterson's voice was shrill. "No one was supposed to be killed!"

Xuan slowly turned to face him, bringing a folding stock M-25 out from under his long coat. "I'm stealing a Trident missile, you fool."

"But, you can't do that!" Patterson cried.

"Who is going to stop me?" Xuan smiled, aiming the muzzle of the assault rifle at his chest. "You and your pathetic little bunch of misfits?"

The M-25 spat a three-round burst. Patterson took all

16

three rounds in the chest and crumpled to the ground. He raised himself on one arm, blood running from the corner of his mouth. "Why?" he gasped.

Without saying a word, Xuan raised the assault rifle to his shoulder to take careful aim and pulled the trigger. The bullet hit Patterson between the eyes, exploding the back of his head.

Xuan turned to the four Boa Hoa commandos who had detached themselves from the main group and were approaching him. "Kill them all," he ordered in Vietnamese, pointing to the six stunned members of M.E.L.A. who had stopped the train in the name of peace, love, and brotherhood.

The high mountain forest rang with high-pitched screams and the rattle of automatic weapons fire.

The blue and white Bell Jet Ranger helicopter skimmed over the tops of the towering fir trees and pulled up for another pass over the side of a densely wooded ridge line. As the chopper turned its belly to the sun, the words "King County Sheriff" were visible. In the co-pilot's seat, a sheriff's deputy lowered the field glasses he had been looking through and turned to the pilot.

"Let's take a look at the other side of the ridge," he said. "The south Forest Service road is over there and I think the track runs next to it."

When the weapons train did not make its routine radio call to check in with the local authorities whose territory it was passing through, the chopper had been sent to look for it. The deputy took off his cap and wiped his forehead, the morning sun streaming through the chopper's canopy had warmed the cockpit.

"Stupid damn map," he muttered, shaking his head. "If they're going to send us all the way out here to look for a lost train, for Christ's sakes, the least they can do is give us a map that a man can read."

The problem wasn't the map, the pilot could have told him that. The problem was that the deputy simply couldn't read the damned thing. The pilot shrugged. It was all the same to him if they ever found that train or not, he was flying and he loved to fly. Also, this was the best time of the year to fly in the Pacific Northwest. Not even a wisp of a cloud marred the china blue sky and the morning breeze was blowing the gray-brown Seattle smog out to sea. To the south, the distant, snow-shrouded top of Mount Rainier loomed majestically from a sea of dark green forest like a huge soft ice cream cone. It was a perfect day to be in the air.

Lining up on the right side of the ridge, the pilot gently pushed forward on the cyclic control and rolled back on the throttle as he dropped the collective. The old Jet Ranger swooped down for another run above the treetops.

In the rear compartment, a county paramedic who liked to ride along with the chopper just in case they came across someone who needed his first aid services, was also scanning the trees through field glasses. "Hey!" he shouted to the pilot over the intercom. "Over to the left! There it is!"

The pilot snapped his head to the left. It did look like there was a break in the dense forest, but it was hard to tell. Pushing down on the rudder pedal, he banked the Jet Ranger to the left for a closer look. The deputy focused his glasses and scanned the area. He saw it.

He pushed the transmission button on the radio microphone and was bringing it up to his lips just as a figure dressed in camouflage clothing stepped out from under the trees at the edge of the rail right of way. The figure raised a dark tube to his shoulder and aimed it at the helicopter.

"Oh shit!" the deputy yelled, unaware that he was still holding the transmission switch down on the microphone. "Look out! He's got a Goddamn missile . . ."

The pilot, a veteran of the Nicaraguan War of 1992, had also seen the man with the missile launcher. Instinctively, he stomped down on the rudder pedal and slammed the cyclic control all the way over, throwing the helicopter into a sudden, hard banked turn. But it was too late.

A trail of dirty white smoke streaked up into the air and followed the Jet Ranger as it frantically tried to escape. A second later a blinding explosion ripped the chopper apart.

The shock waves gently rippled the treetops as burning fragments of men and their machine fell into the trees at the bottom of the canyon to the left of the rail line.

Xuan slowly smiled as he lowered the stolen U.S. Army Viper anti-aircraft missile launcher from his shoulder. It had been almost too easy, he thought, the missile was as good as the colonel had said it was. He turned back into the trees and motioned to a group of six men dressed in camouflage uniforms and red berets.

"Di-Di," he ordered them to move out in Vietnamese.

The other members of the Boa Hoa, a gang of Vietnamese criminals led by the man who had told Patterson about the weapons train, returned to the task at hand, loading the nuclear warhead of a Trident missile into the bed of the four-wheel-drive pickup. As soon as it was tied down securely, Xuan and half of his men got into the truck and drove off. As the pickup started down the Forest Service road, a tall column of greasy black smoke rose slowly up into the cool morning air over the Cascade Mountains, staining the china blue sky.

It was no longer a perfect day for flying.

A little less than an hour later, a helicopter flew through the clear skies high over Seattle's waterfront. This time, her skin was dark police blue and the yellow letters U.S.T.P.F. could be clearly seen along her flanks. A small American flag was painted on her shark-like tail fin and the number ten was printed on her nose in big white numbers. In the cockpit of the Griffin, Mugabe watched the harbor below and occasionally glanced over at the array of sensor instruments on the console to his left. He shook his head and keyed his throat mike.

"We've got to go around again, Wolfman," he said over the intercom. "It's still not reading right."

Rick Wolff grinned slowly under his helmet visor. "No problem, Mojo," he answered. "I'd rather be up here than sitting on the ramp waiting for something to happen. You want to make another pass or go back and have Red take another look?"

Mugabe made another adjustment and looked up from the sensor panel. "I think I can get it if we try it one more time."

"Roger that," Wolff said as he banked the sleek dark blue Griffin over on her side and snapped her tail around for another flight over the harbor. The two TPF officers were trying to calibrate their ship's sensors by taking readings from the infra-red emissions of the hydrofoil ferries and hovercraft water taxies crowding the busy Seattle waterfront. It was a routine job, but one that they had to finish before they would be completely ready for action.

They had just started their second pass when their flight helmet earphones burst into life. "Dragon One Zero, this is Dragon Control, come in."

Wolff squeezed the radio transmission switch in his collective control stick and answered. "Control, this is One Zero, what's up?"

"Control," came the raspy voice of an older woman over the radio. "Command One wants you to break off what you're doing and report to the King County Sheriff's Department at North Bend ASAP."

"What's the big hurry, Mom?" Wolff asked, punching the name North Bend into his navigational computer so the location would come up on his electronic map. TPF Sergeant Ruby Jenkins was the brains and voice of Dragon Control, the dispatch center for the Griffins of Dragon Flight. Sergeant Jenkins was affectionately known to the pilots as Mom, but she ruled her electronic kingdom with an iron hand.

"Control, you'll be briefed when you get there, but they think that one of their choppers has just been shot down."

"Shot down?" Wolff repeated quickly. "What the hell's going on?"

"One Zero, this is Control," the woman's voice was sharp. "Do I have to remind you of proper radio procedures again? This is not a secure channel."

"One Zero, keep your knickers on, Mom. I was just trying to find out what you're getting us into. Mugabe's still working with that new sensor head."

"Dragon One Zero," came a deep male voice over their

20

headsets. "This is Command One, what's your status?"

Wolff glanced over to his co-pilot who gave him a thumbs up. "This is One Zero, we're go now."

"Command One copy," Buzz answered. "You two cowboys had better get your act together and get moving."

"Command One, this is One Zero, copy. We are Code Zero now." Wolff radioed back letting their captain know that he was scrambled for that location. He glanced down at his watch. "Our Echo Tango Alpha is sixteen minutes."

"Control clear."

Mugabe looked over at the Wolfman. "What's Buzz got his dick in a knot about this time?"

"Beats me," Wolff shrugged. "And Mom didn't sound too happy either."

The pilot twisted the throttle of the Griffin's twin turbines all the way over against the stop and watched the turbine RPM needles bury themselves against the pegs. He didn't know what the problem was, but at over 250 miles an hour, it wouldn't be long before he found out.

CHAPTER 3

North Bend, Washington

The King County sheriff's heliport in the little town of
North Bend was in a state of utter chaos when Wolff flared
out and brought the sleek Griffin in for a landing. Patrol cars
were skidding to a halt in the gravelled parking lot. Armed
police in tactical uniforms and assault rifles were climbing
into four-wheel-drive vehicles and racing off. Several helicopters, both State Police and U.S. Forest Service, were standing
by, their rotors turning.

Usually when he had a captive audience like this, Wolff
liked to make a dramatic landing. Swooping down out of the
sky in his powerful machine and hauling up on the collective
at the last possible moment, he would flare out mere inches
off the ground. It was a maneuver guaranteed to impress the
locals as well as scaring the hell out of them. But with all the
confusion today, he thought he'd better keep a cool tool until
he found out what was going on.

Opening the cockpit doors, he and Mugabe stepped out
onto the ground just as a sheriff's deputy raced up, crouching
over to clear the Griffin's still spinning rotor blades. "The
sheriff wants to see you right away," he shouted over the dying
whine of the twin turbines.

The two chopper cops followed the deputy into the Sheriff's
Department building and were led into a crowded operations
room. Sheriff's deputies, state policemen and forest rangers
were all clustered around a big map on the wall. "Here he is,
Sheriff," the deputy said as he led Wolff over to the group.

A heavy-set man in a police khaki uniform turned to face

22

the pilot. The brown cowboy boots and black western hat reminded Wolff of a traditional sheriff of the "Old West," but the 10mm Glock automatic pistol resting in his quick draw leather told Wolff that this was not some country rube. This was one local law enforcement officer who was not behind the times. The powerful Glock was also the preferred man-stopper of the TPF.

" 'Bout time," the sheriff growled around the end of the cigar clenched in his teeth as he extended his hand. "Buck Jones, I'm the sheriff around here."

Wolff took his hand. "Tac Force Flight Sergeant Rick Wolff and this is my partner, Flight Officer Mugabe. What seems to be the problem, Sheriff?"

The sheriff glanced at Wolff's long dark blond hair and the co-pilot's shaved head, bushy mustache and the small gold earring. The peace officer shook his head. These were the federal super cops he'd been hearing about? Christ, they looked more like drug dealers dressed in blue flight suits. He took the cigar from his mouth.

"The problem is that a White Train transporting nuclear missiles failed to make its routine check-in call. Figuring that it'd had some kind of breakdown, I sent a chopper up to look for it and it got shot down."

"White Train?" Wolff asked, unfamiliar with the slang the sheriff used.

"That's what we call the trains that carry the Trident missiles to the Navy sub base at Bangor."

"When did this happen?"

"Little over an hour ago," the sheriff answered grimly.

Wolff made his way over to the big topographic map on the wall. "Okay, let's start from the beginning and you tell me everything you know."

"We get notified whenever one of these trains is due to come through the county so we can keep an eye out in case the local anti-nuke freaks want to play silly games. Anyway, they carry their own MP security unit on board, so all we do is monitor the radio and they check in every half hour. The last call we got from them was at nine and they were here." The sheriff pointed to a spot deep in the National Forest.

"When they didn't make their scheduled nine-thirty call, we tried to contact them, but they didn't answer."

He paused for a moment and looked out of the window to the heliport.

"Anyway," he continued. "Right after ten this morning, we still hadn't been able to get through to them, so I sent one of my deputies, Williams, up in a chopper to find out what the problem was. 'Bout a half an hour later, I got part of a radio message from him. Or at least I think it was from him."

"What do you mean?" Wolff asked.

"Someone was yelling about a missile," Jones answered. "And then he was cut off."

Wolff glanced over to his partner. The shipment of stolen military weapons that Dragon Flight had been sent to track down had included several of the Army's potent new XM-104 Viper shoulder-fired anti-aircraft missiles. If the sheriff's chopper had been hit with a Viper, this was their first lead on the stolen weaponry.

"Show me where this happened."

Jones studied the map. "We got a call from the chopper just a few minutes before it went down." He pointed to an area of hills and forest to the south of the rail line. "And the pilot said that he thought they were right about here."

The sheriff looked embarrassed. "Williams was having a little trouble with his map," he explained.

Wolff took the digital note pad from the leg pocket of his flight suit and noted the map coordinates. "You think this is somehow connected to the train going off the air?"

The sheriff shrugged. "I don't know, but we've never had trouble with these trains before."

"You have any ground units out now?" he asked.

The sheriff consulted the map and pointed. "I've got six men in two four-by-fours headed up there. They should be on this road going east."

"What radio frequency and call sign are they using?"

"Our normal one, channel two, and the call sign is King Mobile."

Wolff noted the information and put the pad back. "Okay, here's the drill. My partner and I are going to call this in to

24

our headquarters and then we're going to go check that area out. Tell your people that we'll be on their frequency. Our call sign is Dragon One Zero."

Wolff locked eyes with the sheriff. "Since this is a federal matter now, the TPF will be in command of your ground units in the area. Do you have any problems with that?"

The sheriff paused. "No," he said, shaking his head. "There won't be any problems, just keep me informed."

"You got it, Sheriff. We'll take off right now."

Motioning for Mugabe to follow him, Wolff made his way back out to his ship and climbed on board.

"For a moment there, I thought that you were going to have to lean on that guy a little," Mugabe laughed as he strapped himself into his seat and started the take-off checklist.

Wolff glanced over at his co-pilot as he tightened his shoulder harness. "Not really," he said. "It's just that some of these local boys don't like the idea of turning control of an operation over to the feds. It doesn't look good to the citizens when the next election rolls around."

"Do you think it was one of those stolen Vipers that got his chopper?"

Wolff shrugged. "I don't know, man. But, if it was, we've got our work cut out for us."

"No shit."

The XM-104 Viper was the latest in a series of American shoulder-fired anti-aircraft missiles dating back to the XM-41 Redeye of the 1960s. Compared to the primitive heat-seeking Redeye, the Viper was the Rolls-Royce of modern anti-aircraft missiles. Guided to the target with a laser designator, the Viper accelerated to Mach 2 just a hundred meters out of the launcher. By the time a pilot saw the flare of the missile's launch charge, he barely had time to blink before he was blown out of the sky. If the missing Vipers had gotten into the hands of criminals, even the Tac Force Griffins were going to find it difficult to survive in the same airspace with them.

As soon as Wolff pulled pitch to the rotor blades and the sleek Griffin lifted off, he banked the machine to the east toward the mountains. "I'd better let Buzz know what we've got here," he said, triggering the switch to the throat mike of his helmet. "Dragon Control, this is Dragon One Zero."

"Dragon Control," came Mom's voice over the headphones. "Go."

"One Zero, let me speak to Command One."

Buzz quickly came on the radio. "Command One, go ahead."

"One Zero, we've got a real problem here." Wolff quickly briefed him on the situation they were facing. ". . . and we are enroute now to check out the last reported position of the chopper."

"Command One," Buzz radioed back. "I am dispatching Dragon One Four Code Zero to your Code One. Wait till they arrive."

"One Zero, copy. Anything further?"

"Negative, Dragon Control clear."

Wolff glanced down at the map coordinates on his digital knee pad and banked the chopper a little more to the east.

"Didn't Buzz just tell us to wait for Gunner and Legs to show up?" Mugabe asked.

"Yeah." Wolff's face broke into a slow, boyish grin. "But he didn't say where we had to wait. I'm going to wait for them in the search area."

"Buzz is going to have our asses for this." Mugabe shook his head.

"Not if we get those suckers."

"Don't forget they probably have a Viper," Mugabe reminded him.

The grin abruptly left Wolff's face. "That's why I want to make sure that we get there first," he said grimly. "I want to take that thing out before One Four shows up and gets in my road."

Mugabe didn't say anything more as they flew deeper into the forest; he knew what was running through his partner's mind. This was another chance to put it all on the line again and win. Rick Wolff had a real give-a-shit attitude about almost everything in life except flying and winning. When it came to those two subjects, the Wolfman could get downright serious. Mugabe shook his head; the captain was going to have a fit about this.

"Okay, what's the plan?" he asked.

"Well, Mojo," Wolff's grin was back. "We're just going to sneak up on those scumbags and blow them away."

"What about the good guys who are supposed to be on that train?"

The pilot turned and gave Mugabe a wide grin. "You're just going to have to be careful not to hit any of 'em, aren't you? Real careful."

As soon as the Griffin was within two miles of the last reported position of the downed chopper, Wolff snapped his face shield down and tightened his shoulder harness. It was time to get serious.

"Okay, Mojo, let's go full defensive," he ordered his co-pilot.

In the left seat, Mugabe snapped his own face shield down as his fingers danced over his weapons and counter measure controls. If there was a Viper active in the area, they were going to need all the help they could get.

One of the switches he flipped controlled the "Mirror Skin" on the Griffin, a counter-measure designed to change the color of the Griffin's skin and to defeat laser guided missiles. A minute amount of electric current was sent through the chopper's outer skin and excited the di-electric molecules of the special dark blue paint, increasing its reflective index by five thousand percent. From the ground, it looked like the chopper had been instantly coated with a solid sheet of bright blue mirrored glass.

The mirror skin would make it more difficult for the missile to achieve a laser lock-on by deflecting and scattering the laser light beam, but it was not insurance against being shot down. Not only did the Viper use a laser guidance system, it had an infra-red back-up system as well. Their chopper was not fitted with the Black Hole IR suppression kits on the turbine exhausts, so they were still vulnerable to the missile's heat-seeking back up guidance system.

The Viper had been designed to be used by a soldier with little or no training with the system, but he was counting on his opponent not being familiar enough with the missile to use it to its greatest advantage. If they were lucky, they would be able to spot the launcher's laser signature and take it out before the Viper got an IR lock-on and fired.

If Wolff had been willing to wait for the second chopper, the two Griffins could have paired up to work together as a hunter-killer team. One of them would have served as bait, a target for the laser beam while the other one fired as soon as the laser designator came on. That was the textbook way to deal with this situation.

But as always, Wolff was in a hurry, so he and his partner were going to try to do it the hard way.

Mugabe had no problem spotting the train. His target acquisition radar easily picked up the immobile mass of steel sitting on the track. It also picked up the twisted wreckage of the sheriff's chopper in the bottom of the canyon. He quickly keyed the grid coordinates of the wreck into the computer so he could guide the ground units into the area later.

Now that they had located the target area, Wolff banked away to hide behind a nearby hill mass while he consulted his terrain radar readout. It had been a little over an hour since the chopper had been shot down and the pilot had no idea whether the guy with the missile launcher was still in the area or not. The only safe thing to do, however, was to assume that he was and that he had another Viper.

"I'm going to poke my head up to take a look," Wolff said. "You ready?"

"Do it."

Mugabe bent over his sensors as the chopper cleared the top of the hill. Not only was he looking for a laser designator, but he was also watching his doppler radar readout looking for signs of movement in the forests below.

"I've got a faint doppler reading in the sector to the north of the track," Mugabe said tensely.

"Roger." Wolff brought the Griffin back down under cover behind the hill and checked his terrain-following radar again for the best way to get to the target without exposing them to the Viper. He traced a route through the surrounding hills that would keep them under cover until they reached a good firing position.

"Hang on, Mojo," he said. "We're going in."

CHAPTER 4

Snoqualmie National Forest

Nguyen To Phu cocked his head; he thought he had heard something. "Quiet!" he hissed, jumping to his feet.

The Vietnamese strained his ears, but heard nothing. This had happened several times before this morning, the densely forested hills did strange things to sound. Not only did the trees muffle sound, sometimes the hills would echo a noise from miles away. It was probably just another one of the four-wheel-drive vehicles that had been driving through on the Forest Service road a half a mile to the north.

He glanced down at his watch again, counting the minutes until he and his four man security team would be free to leave. Xuan had ordered them to stay with the train and cover his withdrawal until the pickup carrying the Trident warhead could get all the way out of the National Forest and lose itself in the Seattle-bound traffic on US highway 90. It had taken far longer than Xuan had planned to break into the freight car carrying the Trident missiles and dismantle one of the warheads.

This was why they'd had to shoot down that country sheriff's helicopter when it had suddenly appeared overhead. Dong had not wanted to draw attention to their operation, but when the chopper appeared, the job wasn't done and they couldn't take a chance of it radioing the train's location to its headquarters.

Phu always faithfully obeyed the orders of his superiors in the Boa Hoa; to do otherwise meant a long and painful death, but he didn't like being in the forbidding forest. He was a city-

30

bred man from the old Vietnamese imperial capital of Hue and had never been in the jungles that his country was so famous for. The crowded, violent back alleys of Seattle's "Little Saigon" were like a second home to him, but the dark, peaceful mountain forests made him nervous.

He knew, though, there was little chance that anyone would drive up the faint trail leading to this spot. And with the Viper missiles, there was no chance that a plane was going to report them either. A plane might find them, but it would not have time to send a radio message before he blasted it out of the sky. In just another half hour they would be free to follow their leader back to Seattle.

Phu checked again to make sure that the missile launcher lying across his lap was still switched to the active targeting mode. It was. The instruction manual that had come with the missile explained that the Viper would warm up and be ready to fire in under two seconds, but he didn't want to take any chances. If another plane suddenly appeared overhead, he wanted to be able to shoot it down instantly, so he left the missile switched on.

"I'm picking up a strange reading here," Mugabe reported, looking up from his sensor readouts. "On a bearing of two three zero. It looks almost like someone is 'painting' the tree-tops with a laser designator."

"That's got to be our man," Wolff grinned behind his face shield. He felt the adrenaline start racing through his body and he tightened his fingers around the cyclic and collective controls. He loved the blood-singing, gut-tightening feeling that came every time he pitted his flying skills against a worthy opponent. He hoped, however, that this guy wasn't too good. Just good enough to make it interesting.

"I can't figure out what he's doing, though," Mugabe frowned. "Unless he's playing around with that thing. It's like he's got it switched on active mode and is sighting it in on a tree or something like that."

"Whatever he's doing," Wolff said, watching the attack screen on the HUD for the readout on the laser's location so he could come in behind it. "Let's kick his ass and get this over with."

The pilot was just reaching down to turn the wick up and go into his attack when the earphones in his helmet burst into life.

"Dragon One Zero, this is One Four, we are enroute to your location, Echo Tango Alpha Six Zero."

"Oh shit," Wolff muttered as he triggered his throat mike. "Dragon One Four, this is One Zero, stand clear," he warned the other TPF Griffin chopper that Buzz had sent to help them. "We are Code Twenty, I say again Code Twenty. We've got an active Viper missile in this sector. Go to full defensive, Gunner, get under cover and stay out of the way till we can take care of this guy."

"Need an assist?" TPF Flight Sergeant Daryl Jennings radioed back. Code Twenty meant that a police unit was engaged and, if there was shooting going on, "Gunner" Jennings wanted to be right in the middle of it. He never passed up a chance to "pop caps" on the bad guys.

"Negative, negative," Wolff almost yelled. That was all he needed right now, one of Gunner's crazy Banzai gunship runs right down that guy's throat, guns blazing.

"That missile's hot and running. I'm in position to get him, but if you show up he'll nail your ass before you can get a shot off. Switch to Tac Link One so I can download the target data to you."

"Copy, switching to Tac Link One now," Jennings reported back.

The Griffin's on-board computers could "talk" to one another and, in the Tactical Linkup mode, Wolff could send all of his target and sensor data to the other ship with the electronic speed of light. That way, when he made his attack, the other chopper could "see" everything he was doing. If Wolff did something wrong and got blasted out of the sky, it would instantly show up on Jennings' tactical monitor and he could plan his attack accordingly.

Jennings came back on the air a second later. "We're linked," he said. "Go for it."

"Roger," Wolff answered.

Mugabe's fingers tightened on his firing controls for the weapons in the nose turret as Wolff pulled pitch to the rotor blades. The shark-like Griffin lifted out from behind the hill that had been shielding them from the target. Since they had not known that they would be going to war against a military anti-aircraft missile, the Griffin was not carrying her optional, long range 25mm Chain gun in the turret. All she had was her short range, light 7.62mm Chain gun and the even shorter ranged 40mm grenade launcher to fight with. But if they were lucky, that would be enough to do the job.

If they were lucky.

Mugabe selected the six round burst mode on the 7.62mm and dialed stun gas cartridges into the ammo feed belt for the 40mm. He could hardly use the full 900 round per minute from the Chain gun or the HE grenades from the 40mm in a possible hostage situation like this. As it was, if the bad guys were using the train crew for cover he was taking a chance using even the six-round burst, but they were going up against a missile. Single shots just wouldn't do it and the stun gas didn't take effect fast enough to keep the gunner from launching the missile.

This time, they were going to have to shoot to kill and sort the bodies out later.

While Dragon One Four stayed safely behind the cover of a hilltop well over a mile away, in the left seat, Flight Officer Sandra Revell held her breath as she stared at the tactical HUD screen in front of her.

With the two Griffins linked, she could see the Viper's laser designator and the position of Wolff's Griffin. Wolff was attacking from behind the missile gunner, but she knew that with the missile "hot" and tracking, it would only take a split second for him to spin around and launch it. Wolff and Mugabe would only have one chance to take him out before the deadly missile blew them out of the sky. But Revell knew that if any chopper jocks in the entire TPF could pull this one off, it was Rick the Wolfman and his gunner Mojo Mugabe. The two flyers were aerial legends in the Tac Force and they had won the TPF "Top Gun" aerial weapons and tactics competition for the last three years running.

Sandra knew that Wolff and Mugabe were the best there was, but she still concentrated on the display on her attack screen ready do battle herself. There was always the chance that the Wolfman's luck would run out and she and Jennings would have to take out the target.

Nguyen To Phu leaped to his feet when he caught the sound of the Griffin's rotors coming up behind him. Where had that damned helicopter come from?

Phu spun around to face it, but in his haste, he fumbled as he swung the Viper launcher up to his shoulder. He glanced down to make sure that the launch safety was off and, in that split second, he died.

Mugabe's first six-round burst from the 7.62mm was right on target. Three of the rounds hit the Vietnamese in the upper torso. The light caliber rounds, however, did not impart enough kinetic energy to the target when they hit to knock him over. Reflexively, he squeezed the launch trigger on the Viper and the missile fired.

"Launch! Launch!" Mugabe yelled. His finger stabbed at the decoy flare launch button on the counter-measures panel.

At this range, they only thing that would save them was if he could get the heat-seeking guidance system on the missile to lock-on to a decoy flare. The flare burned at ten thousand degrees, a hundred times as hot at the turbine exhausts of the Griffin. When the missile's guidance system saw the hotter flares, it would track them instead of following the helicopter.

Wolff caught a glimpse of the Viper's smoke trail as he slammed the Griffin over onto its side, putting the chopper's belly to the missile. The violent maneuver unloaded the rotor head causing the blades to lose lift. The Griffin dropped like a stone. Wolff dumped his collective to bring the rotor RPM back up and dropped his nose right as the Viper flashed by, its IR heat-seeking warhead locked-on to one of the decoy flares.

The speeding missile missed them by mere inches and exploded harmlessly.

The pilot righted his ship and jerked up on the collective control, pulling pitch to the rotor blades. The spinning blades caught the cool mountain air and gave the chopper lift. Wolff pulled up right above the treetops.

"Jesus!" Mugabe let the breath out he had been holding. "That was close!"

"Too fucking close," Wolff snapped as he banked the chopper around for another gun run. "Keep your finger on the trigger. I'm going back down there and see if anyone else wants to play stupid games."

Mugabe swung the turret over to the left as the Griffin swooped down low over the top of the halted train. Now that Wolff had taken out the Viper, Dragon One Four joined up with him in case there was anyone else in the area who wanted to try their chances against a Griffin. He slid in a few hundred meters behind Wolff's ship to cover him.

One of Phu's men foolishly stepped out from behind a tree as Wolff's Griffin flashed past, and fired a quick burst from his assault rifle at the speeding chopper. He didn't get a chance to fire again, however. Sandra Revell triggered a long burst from her 7.62mm Chain gun and added several rounds of stun gas from the grenade launcher. The gunman went down in a crumpled heap.

"Thanks, Legs," Wolff radioed back to the second chopper.

"Anytime, Wolfman," Revell replied, scanning the tree line for more trouble.

Jennings flew top cover while Wolff made a slow pass low over the train. "It looks like one of the freight cars has been broken into," he observed.

"You'd better call it in," Mugabe answered. "If they got to one of those Trident missiles, we've got big problems."

At that moment, Wolff spotted the bodies of Patterson and the rest of his Mother Earth Liberation Army members sprawled out under the fir trees.

"Oh shit," he said, his hand automatically reaching for the switch to his throat mike. "We've got to get those sheriff's deputies up here ASAP."

Wolff and Jennings continued to fly top cover over the disabled train until the first of the sheriff's vehicles arrived on the scene. Even though Wolff had radioed that the situation was under control, the deputies piled out of their truck with their weapons at the ready. They were taking no chances.

As soon as the deputies radioed that the area was secure, Wolff set his Griffin down on the rail tracks in front of the train. Stepping out onto the ground, he drew the Glock 10mm pistol from his shoulder holster. Revell had dusted the area with stun gas, but he was taking no chances either. Not with people who shot missiles at helicopters.

The pistol was unnecessary, however, except for the three men still unconscious from the gas; the rest of the gang were dead.

"What've we got here?" he asked one of the deputies.

The man rolled Phu's body over with his boot. "He looks Vietnamese," he said.

Wolff noted the man's bloodstained camouflage uniform and the red beret lying on the ground. "Some kind of private army?" he asked.

"Hard to say," the deputy shrugged. "We've had so much trouble with these Asian gangs that it's hard to the tell the players without a scorecard."

"What's the story on the civilian bodies?" the pilot asked.

"Just dumb college kids," the deputy shook his head. "One of them had some flyers in his backpack saying something about the Mother Earth Liberation Army. Another bunch of anti-nuke, environmentalists."

"What's the connection with the Vietnamese?" Wolff asked.

"Beats the hell outa me."

Wolff reached down, picked up the Viper launcher and slung it over his shoulder. Back at the TOC, they could check the serial number against the list of stolen weapons and determine where it had come from. There was no doubt in his mind, however, that the launcher was from the missing shipment they had been sent to track down.

Just then, Mugabe stepped out from behind the train, his face was ashen. "Wolfman!" he called out. "Over here! The missile's gone."

CHAPTER 5

TPF Tactical Operations Center, Seattle

When Wolff had called in the information about the missing Trident missile nuclear warhead, the Tactical Police Force TOC at the Coast Guard Station almost exploded with shock. Captain Buzz Corcran made the pilot repeat the message to make sure that he had all the information before he laid down the microphone.

"Oh sweet Jesus," he said softly, closing his eyes for a short moment. "Not a nuke."

What had started out to be a routine assignment for Dragon Flight had suddenly turned into a federal police officer's worst nightmare: a nuclear threat at the hands of criminals.

As Buzz quickly collected his thoughts, his hand automatically went to his left shirt pocket, but it was empty. He shook his head and wished for the hundredth time that he hadn't stopped smoking.

The problem was that he couldn't stand those new, no-cancer-causing things that were called cigarettes nowadays. They were the only cigarettes you could legally buy and he hated them. They tasted so bad that he had quit smoking completely rather than switching over to them. At a time like this, however, he would have gladly settled for even one of those foul-tasting things. Old habits die hard.

Buzz let his hand fall back and turned around in his chair. "Ruby," he said. "Patch me into the Denver Operations Center."

"You want it on the scrambler?"

"Good Christ yes!" Buzz exploded. "If one word of this gets out, we'll have a complete panic on our hands. This whole place will turn into a ghost town overnight and we'll really be in the shit."

This was not the first time that the Dragon Flight Commander had faced this kind of potential disaster, but he had never gotten used to the political pressure that he knew was going to come with it.

The Tactical Police Force had been a political hot potato from its very inception in 1996. Back in the mid-1990s, it had become all too apparent that America was losing the war against crime. The efforts of the existing federal law enforcement organizations, the FBI, the Federal Marshals, the DEA, the Sky Marshals, the Customs Police, and the Immigration Service were not enough to contain the growing crime wave. The primary reason that they had failed was that too often their efforts were scattered and uncoordinated and they were not organized or equipped to deal with criminal gangs that had evolved into small, well-armed private armies. The situation was critical and something had to be done.

What was needed to solve the problem was one unified, well equipped federal police organization that would combine the law enforcement functions of all of the old organizations under one command. Initially, there had been a great deal of resistance to this idea, particularly from the professional liberals and entrenched corrupt public officials. The political battles had raged for months. But this was an idea whose time had clearly come. The old methods were not working and the fabric of national life was in danger of being shredded by the crime lords and their gangs. It was time that the citizens took the country back from the criminal elements.

One of President Bush's last official acts at the end of his second term had been to sign the Federal Tactical Police Force Act that created the United States Tactical Police Force. Under the provisions of the act, the TPF was given the authority to preserve the peace and uphold the law anywhere in the fifty-two United States.

The Tac Force had the mission and they did the job. They

did their job well too, but there was still a great deal of political sharpshooting at them from all levels of government. Particularly during an operation involving something as serious as this.

There were dozens of congressmen who would like nothing more than to see the Tac Force fall flat on its collective ass. According to Denver, Buzz only had a few hours, a day at the most, before the politicians would start screaming that the TPF had failed to protect the American people and demanding that they be pulled out of Seattle.

Buzz knew that if he didn't get that stolen warhead back under control ASAP, he would give the Tac Force a black eye that they might never recover from. He also knew that he had to do it before word of the missing nuke was leaked to the press and resulting public panic turned Seattle into a crowd control disaster town. That was something that he was not ready to take the blame for.

"I've got Denver on the scrambler," Ruby said.

Buzz lowered the security screen over his head and started making his report.

As he talked, Lieutenant Phan Le Tran, the commander of the Seattle TPF field office, sat and waited. He had been in the TOC to go over the after-action report on the hovercraft incident with Captain Corcran when the call had come in from Dragon One Zero.

In 1999, the entire west coast of America had an enormous Asian population, and Seattle had the largest of any of the west coast cities. The Northwest had been the final destination for the vast majority of the Hong Kong Chinese who had fled the former British colony when it reverted to the control of the Red Chinese in 1997. Additionally, thousands of Southeast Asian boat people had made it their home over the last three decades of forced migration as well. The fact that, in addition to their commander, over half of the personnel of the Seattle TPF field office were Asian-Americans illustrated the importance of that element of the population in the Pacific Northwest.

Lieutenant Tran was not unaware of the prestige he brought to the Asian community by virtue of being the highest ranking federal cop in Seattle. However, he was also aware that having an Asian cop running the Seattle field office didn't quite balance the negative image of the active Oriental criminal element in Seattle.

When Hong Kong had fallen, not only had wealthy Chinese businessmen fled the Communists, but the old established Hong Kong tongs, the Chinese gangsters, had also found their way to the Northwest. They quickly set up shop and were firmly established in their traditional business of drug dealing, gambling, money-lending and extortion.

The tongs were criminal gangs, but like the established American Mafia, they operated according to a strict "code of honor" and primarily restricted their enterprises to their own sphere of influence: the Asian community. The tongs were lawbreakers, but they were a small problem in comparison to the other Asian criminal element in Seattle, the powerful Vietnamese Boa Hoa gang headed by the infamous ex-North Vietnamese Army Colonel Nguyen Cao Dong.

Unlike the Chinese tongs, the Boa Hoa were completely out of control, they had no criminal "code of honor." Nothing was too violent for them and they did not confine their enterprises to the Asian population. Dong's gang was believed to be responsible for a series of violent bank robberies and a long list of murders. They had also been definitely tied to the lucrative Asian drug trade and high-tech equipment smuggling to the Far East.

Tran and his men had been after Dong for a long time, but so far, the colonel had successfully evaded them. If the sheriff's deputy was right, and the men who had hijacked the train were Vietnamese, Tran was betting that they were part of Dong's operation. No one else could put together an operation like that. A shudder passed through the young Vietnamese cop when he thought of a nuclear weapon being in the hands of a certified maniac like Dong.

He pulled his personal communicator from his belt and punched in the number for his own operations sergeant. If he got his men out on the street fast enough, maybe they would pick up something on this latest Boa Hoa incident and get a handle on it before things got totally out of control.

When Buzz finished his scrambled call to the TPF Regional Headquarters at Denver, he looked drained. "Denver's completely upside down about this," he said wearily. "I've been on the horn all the way back to headquarters in Washington. We've got to recover that damned thing yesterday."

"What do you want me to tell Wolff and Jennings?" Ruby asked, reminding him that two of his Griffins were still on the scene.

"Denver's getting in touch with the nuke weapons people and I want Jennings to stay there till they relieve him. They'll secure the site and conduct their own investigation. I want Wolfman to bring the suspects back here so we can get started on this ASAP."

Ruby keyed her throat mike. "Dragon One Zero," she radioed. "This is Control."

"One Zero," Wolff answered. "Go ahead."

"This is Control, switch to Scramcom One."

Wolff switched his radio over to the scrambled tactical communications channel. "One Zero, go on Scramcom One."

"This is Control," Ruby answered. "Command One has notified the Nuclear Weapons Commission and they have a security team on the way to your location to take over from the King County sheriff's department. He wants One Four to remain on station until they arrive while you take custody of the suspects and return them to this location ASAP."

"One Zero, copy. How 'bout the bodies?"

Ruby looked up at Buzz. "They can't tell us much," he shrugged.

"This is Control, leave them for the security unit to transport later."

"One Zero, copy."

"Jesus," Buzz said, rubbing the back of his neck. "A fucking stolen nuke."

Twenty minutes later, Wolff brought his Griffin in for a flashy landing at the Coast Guard station, dropping down so fast that the skids kissed the tarmac before he pulled the nose

41

up sharply and flared out to kill his momentum.

"Red's going to kill you if you bend his bird," Mugabe cautioned as Wolff taxied the hovering chopper over to the refueling point.

"Never happen," the pilot said with a big grin. His fingers flew over the switches as he killed the power to the twin General Electric T-700 turbines. The whine died and, overhead, the four bladed rotor coasted to a stop as the two men opened their cockpit doors and stepped out onto the tarmac.

Armed guards from Lieutenant Tran's Seattle field office were waiting to take the two prisoners into custody to start their interrogation. One of the advantages of having so many Asian cops in the Seattle office was that they had a multitude of linguists who spoke any of over a dozen Oriental languages that could be heard in the streets of Seattle. If these guys knew anything, Tran would find it out ASAP.

As soon as the Vietnamese prisoners were taken away, Mugabe turned to go. "You get the gas," the co-pilot said, starting for the TPF hangar. "I'm going see the ordnance men about rearming."

"You got it," Wolff said, opening the fuel filler door on the side of the Griffin and reaching for the JP-4 jet fuel refueling nozzle.

While the JP-4 was pumping into the nearly empty fuel tanks of Wolff's Griffin, TPF Sergeant Eric Larsen, known in Dragon Flight as "Eric the Red" or simply "Red," walked up to the chopper.

Larsen was the Dragon Flight maintenance officer and the crew chief for Dragon One Zero. Red's love affair with helicopters had begun back when he had been a young chopper mechanic in Vietnam. When he had gotten out of the Army, he had started working on both commercial and police choppers and now, almost thirty years later, he was still in love with rotary wing flying machines.

Red was a big, burly, softspoken man who looked every one of his fifty-odd years, but the remnants of his once flaming red hair served as a warning of his hot temper. When the Griffin was still on the drawing boards, Red had provided the Bell design team with much valuable information as to what a real police helicopter ought to be as only a man of his years of experience would know.

As a result, Red considered the Griffins to be his children and woe be unto any young hotshot pilot who abused one of his birds.

"You two maniacs get anymore holes shot in this thing?" he asked Wolff.

"Not this time," the pilot answered. "But the day isn't over yet, Chief. We've still got a couple hours left. Let me take her up again and I'll see what I can do for you."

Red spat out a piece of the well-chewed cigar he was never without. "You mess with this bird, son," he said softly, his blunt, greasestained finger thumping Wolff on the chest. "And I'm going to talk to Buzz about transferring you two assholes to air traffic control duty keeping track of sea gulls in Bumfuck, Alabama."

"Give me a break, Chief," Wolff protested. "You know I wouldn't do anything to hurt your baby."

"Not unless you want your sex life to suffer," Red answered around the end of his cigar.

"Speaking of my sex life," Wolff grinned. "What's the word about tonight? Has Buzz got us on ramp alert again?"

Red spat another piece of tobacco out of his mouth. "No, you boys lucked out this time, the bozos in One Three have the duty tonight."

Wolff snapped the fuel filler cap door in place and latched the fuel cover door back down. "Bright lights, big city, here I come."

Mugabe walked out of the hangar followed by the ordnance man and a trailer full of ammunition for the empty weapons of the Griffin.

"Hey, Mojo," Wolff yelled over to him. "We've got the night off!"

"Outasight!" The co-pilot grinned broadly. "I'm gonna get right tonight!"

"Not until you hustle your butt and get this bird rearmed," Wolff reminded him. "Buzz will have our ass if we're not topped off and ready to go."

"Then get on it, my man," Mugabe shot back. "And quit

flapping yo lips."

Wolff reached down and unsnapped the latches to the ammunition storage bays in the belly of the Griffin.

"Fill 'er up, regular," he told the ordnance men.

CHAPTER 6

Coast Guard Station

It took the rest of the afternoon before Wolff and Mugabe were finished checking over their helicopter. The Griffin had been designed with low maintenance requirements, but there was still plenty to be done after each mission. As soon as the men were finished, they went to their quarters and changed into civilian clothes before going to the Coast Guard's officer's club for dinner.

Because the Tac Force cops were federal officers, the Coast Guard had given them permission to use their officer's club, but this was the first chance they'd had since they had arrived in Seattle to take advantage of it. Daryl Jennings and his co-pilot Sandra Revell also had the night off and when Wolff and Mugabe entered the club and saw them standing at the bar, they went to join them for a drink.

Not surprisingly, a flock of young Coast Guard officers crowded around the tall, blonde Revell. Wolff noticed that she was in her party clothes tonight, her long hair was down and she was wearing a pair of skin-tight pants.

"Hey! Legs," the pilot called out, elbowing his way through the crowd to her side. "How 'bout you and me cruising downtown after dinner and seeing what this burg has to offer in the line of entertainment?"

Sandra turned away from the Coast Guard pilot she had been talking to and slowly looked Wolff up and down. "I'd love to, Wolfman," she said with a sly smile. "But I've got to think of my reputation. You know that a respectable girl like myself just can't afford to be seen with a guy like you."

Sandra's Coast Guard admirers howled at that one.

"A guy like me?" Wolfman cried in mock distress. "What's wrong with me?" This was an old routine with Wolff and Revell. At least once a week, he asked her for a date and every time she turned him down the same way that she turned down offers from all the rest of the other Tac Force cops. Sandra Revell wasn't a nun, she just didn't date the men she worked with.

Sandra raised her eyebrows. "What's wrong with you, Wolff? Well, for one thing, just take a look at that jacket you're wearing."

Wolff looked down at the well worn leather World War II style fighter pilot's jacket he wore. On one breast was sewn a Tac Force Dragon Flight patch, on the other side was the insignia of VMF-214 the Marine fighter squadron that had flown the Corsair to fame in the Pacific in World War Two. He had an American flag sewn on one shoulder and a "Blood Chit" on the back. He looked like an extra in a B grade World War II movie, and that was how he wanted it.

"What's wrong with it?" he asked.

Sandra sniffed. "The men I go out with are somewhat more fashionably dressed."

"Maybe I can borrow a tie from one of these guys," Wolff said, glancing over at the Coast Guardsmen.

"It's more than just the jacket," she smiled. "I don't date cops."

Wolff put his right hand over his heart. "I promise, no shop talk," he said solemnly. "I won't mention any of the many federal statutes that I've sworn to uphold and I won't even talk about the fascinating life I lead as the nation's hottest police chopper pilot."

"You couldn't talk about that anyway, Wolfman," Gunner Jennings broke in. "Unless you're talking about *me*."

Wolff leaned closer to Jennings. "Your ass," he said. "Anyone who knows shit from apple butter knows that I can fly circles around you with a blindfold on."

"Is that what you were doing up there today when that guy took a shot at you?" Gunner said with a grin. "Flying with a blindfold on?"

"What are you talking about?"

"I'm talking about that little dipsy-doo stall you pulled that almost sent you into the trees. What do you call that maneuver anyway?"

"I call it getting my young ass out of the line of fire," Wolff shot back.

"You boys keep out of trouble now," Sandra said as she got up from the bar and took the arm of one of the Coast Guard officers. She had heard about all of this bullshit that she could stand tonight. "The lieutenant here has kindly offered to show me the sights of Seattle."

Both pilots stopped their argument and watched Sandra walk out of the room. Watching the tall blonde cop walk by was always one of the best shows in the Tac Force. Wolff shook his head. "I don't see what she sees in him."

"I don't either," Gunner agreed. "It's got to be the cute white uniform."

"Candy ass."

"Beer," Mojo ordered, ignoring his partner when the bartender appeared.

"Make that two," Wolff said, laying his UNI-CARD on the bar.

"Since you're buying," Gunner said. "I'll have a virgin Marguerita."

The bartender looked puzzled. "Sir?"

"A virgin Marguerita?" Gunner replied. "That's one that hasn't been fucked with. Tequila, lemon juice, but not too much, three ice cubes, a little salt and do not, I say again do not, put it in a blender."

"Right away, sir," the bartender answered.

When the drinks arrived, the three cops took a seat at one of the tables and ordered dinner. "Legs got a little worried about your young ass today, Wolfman," Jennings said after they had given the waitress their orders.

"She sure as hell didn't act like she was concerned about me tonight," Wolff shot back.

"You just don't understand women, man," Mugabe laughed. "She was waiting for you to sweep her off her feet."

"Last time I tried to do that," Wolff said. "Was in the gym

47

and she dropped me flat on my ass."

Both men laughed. Sandra was well known as a tough opponent in hand-to-hand combat exercises.

"Maybe she's looking for a little strange tonight, a walk on the wild side," Mugabe offered.

"At least he's not as strange as some of those FBI guys," Wolff said.

All three Tac Force cops got a good laugh out of that one. The TPF was the youngest of the federal services and the established agencies like the FBI and DEA resented the Tac Force muscling in on what they considered their territory. The Dragon Flight cops, however, didn't really care what the other federal agencies thought about them. The Tac Force had been created to keep that kind of inter-agency back-biting from getting in the way of the war on crime. They knew that they were the elite of the elite and didn't mind letting people know that, once the Tac Force was on the scene.

Their dinner soon arrived and the three men got right to work on it. Dodging Viper missiles was a good way to work up an appetite.

When they had finished, Gunner Jennings glanced over to the bar and spotted several young ladies sipping their drinks and covertly looking around at the Coast Guard officers to see who was watching them.

"Looks like the Coasties really know how to pack them in," he said. "You want to join me at the bar?"

"No, thanks," Wolff replied. "Mojo and I are going to cruise downtown and see the sights."

"It can't get much better than this, guys," Gunner pushed his chair back, eyeing a slim redhead sitting at the end of the bar.

"We'll take our chances."

"I'll catch you gentlemen later," Jennings said as he started for the bar. "I think I'm falling in love."

"The eternal optimist," Wolff observed. "He doesn't realize that they're sharks, slowly circling, looking for a chance to sink their teeth into a nice, steady Coast Guard paycheck."

"We get paid on time," Mojo protested. "We're feds just like the Coasties."

"Yeah," Wolff agreed. "But, we work for a living."

"Right."

"And, we may be the best there is, but we travel all over the damn country enforcing the law and protecting the American way of life, never spending two weeks in the same place."

"We spent the last two weeks in Denver," Mojo pointed out.

"That's what I mean," Wolff grinned. "What woman in her right mind wants to be stuck in Denver while her man is off running around God only knows where chasing down the bad guys?"

"You've got a point," Mojo conceded. "So let's go see if we can rustle up someone who wants to share those few precious hours that we're going to be in town."

"That's the idea," Wolff agreed. He started singing the chorus of a Country and Western classic. "Third Rate Romance, Low Rent Rendezvous."

The two cops walked the short distance back to the hangar where Mugabe had parked his Kawasaki motorcycle. Whenever Dragon Flight was dispatched to a trouble spot in the Western Region, the men and women had to leave their personal automobiles back in Denver. Even so, somehow Mugabe was always able to smuggle his bike onto the C-9 maintenance support transport plane that accompanied the choppers whenever they moved away from their home base.

"It'd be nice if we could work out of Denver once in a while," Wolff said as he reached into the motorcycle's sidecar and pulled out two helmets. "I'd like to have my own wheels for a change."

"Bitch, bitch, bitch," Mugabe laughed, slipping the magnetic coded plastic key into the bike's ignition slot. "You ought to be thankful that Red and I have a good working relationship, otherwise, we'd be walking."

Wolff donned his helmet and slipped down into the low-slung sidecar. "I've almost forgotten what's it's like to ride in a real car."

He had left his other true love, a beat up, deep blue '92 Mazda Miata Turbo roadster parked in the garage of his bachelor's apartment. Someday he hoped that Dragon Flight would get an assignment within driving distance of Denver so he could have the sports car with him. He loved racing around in that little Japanese road rocket.

The Kawasaki started with a powerful purr and Mugabe pulled away from the hangar. At the main gate to the Coast Guard Station, he asked the guard on duty about the local hot spots. The Coast Guardsman thought for a moment before recommending a place several blocks away called the "Happy Hog."

"You'll like it there," he winked. "It's a real meat market on Friday nights."

"Just what I need," Wolff replied. "Hordes of admiring women."

"Just don't tell 'em you're cops," the Coastie advised, eyeing the Dragon Flight patch on Wolff's flight jacket. "Tell 'em that you're pilots or something."

Mugabe laughed. "Yep, that's what we are for sure, my man, pilots or something."

It was a short ride to the "Happy Hog" and the two cops could hear the pounding beat of a western band when they pulled into the parking lot in back. "Nice quiet little place," Wolff remarked as he pulled his helmet off and stashed it back inside the sidecar. "Just what I need to relax after a hard day at the office."

Walking up to the door, Wolff spotted the neon sign on the front of the building, a fat, pink cartoon pig in a cowboy hat laughing his guts out. "This is my kind of place."

He had his hand on the door when he heard a shout from inside. Stepping back out of the way, his right hand automatically went for the .380 Beretta holstered at the back of his belt. He heard an inner door crash open and a deep voice say, ". . . and stay the fuck out!"

Wolff relaxed as the door swung open and a hulking brute in an electric pink, spandex body shirt with a Happy Hog on the front appeared. He had both hands full of a drunk, propelling him through the door, into the street.

"Like I said," Wolff grinned as he reached for the door again. "A nice, quiet little place."

"Are you sure you want to go in there, Wolfman?" Mugabe

asked.

"What's the matter, Mojo, rednecks bother you?"

The co-pilot grinned broadly, the street light glittering on his gold earring and shaved head. "Not as much as I bother them."

Wolff laughed and the two cops walked in together. Like the Coastie had promised, the bar was crowded with good looking women. It was still early, but the holoband was already sweating under the lights of the hologram projector as they tried to play backup for the holo figure of some Country and Western legend.

"Who's he supposed to be?" Mugabe asked.

Wolff looked up and shrugged. "Not sure, Hank Williams Junior or somebody like that."

"Is Hank Williams Junior dead?"

"I don't know."

"If he isn't," Mojo shook his head. "Someone'd better put him out of his misery."

"You just don't appreciate traditional American music."

"You bet your ass I don't."

Wolff spotted an empty table against a wall and made for it. A waitress in tight jeans and a gaudy western shirt came to take their order. "What'll ya have?"

"A draft Lite," Wolff ordered.

"I fancy a mineral water with a slight twist of lime," Mugabe said seriously.

The waitress shook her head and left for the bar. "This isn't California," Wolff warned. "You'd better knock that San Francisco shit off, or you're going to get our asses thrown right out in the street."

"Never to mind, my good fellow," Mugabe replied in a slight British accent. "I have a plan."

Wolff almost didn't want to know what his co-pilot was up to this time. He had learned long ago that Mojo's fake British Empire number was almost as bad as his jive-talking Sixties routine. "And what is this little plan?"

"I say, we came here for a bit of crumpet, what?"

Wolff didn't bother to acknowledge that.

". . . and the best way I know to make sure that we get

51

noticed by the local talent is to offer something different than their usual fare."

"Different? Mineral water and Jolly Old England?"

"Jamaica, my good fellow," Mugabe grinned. "Jamaica."

Wolff shook his head. He could tell that this was going to be another one of those nights and he wasn't sure that he was up to it.

CHAPTER 7

"The Happy Hog Tavern"

Rick Wolff and Jumal Mugabe went back all the way to the inception of the Tac Force Dragon Flight. They had both been in the first Griffin helicopter conversion class and had been assigned to fly together at the start of the weapons training phase.

At first, Wolff hadn't known what to make of the muscular black with the gold earring, the shaved head and the jive-ass attitude. But after the first day on the gunnery range he knew that he was working with a master of aerial weaponry, a real left seat ace.

"Where'd you learn to shoot like that?" he had asked him when they got back to the chopper pad at the end of that first day.

Mugabe rocked back on his heels. "Oh, here and there," he had answered cryptically.

"Here and there where?"

Mojo had flashed a big grin. "Nicaragua, Colombia, Iran, South Africa, places like that."

"Who'd you fly for?"

"Oh, this outfit and that."

"Okay, okay," Wolff laughed. "Why don't I buy you a beer and you can tell me about it."

That night the two men discovered that they had a lot in common besides their love of flying choppers. Wolff had not been able to fly in any of the recent little wars throughout the world, so he was enthralled by Mugabe's war stories. The burly black gunner had flown for several of the government's secret armies as well as for the CIA and DEA. He had finally gotten that out of his system when he had stopped a bullet in the jungles of Honduras and had tried civilian life for a while. Finding that boring, he immediately signed up for the Tac Police when they had started recruiting.

Mojo was very interested to learn that Wolff was a hotrock air show and racing pilot who had a restored World War II vintage F4U-5 Corsair fighter to play with. He immediately volunteered his services if Wolff needed mechanic work done. Among his many talents, Mugabe was also an ace aircraft mechanic and he loved to work on old warbirds.

They also discovered that they both shared the same second hobby, women.

When the Griffin school ended, Wolff requested that Mugabe be assigned as the gunner on his chopper and the two men had worked together ever since. They also spent most of their off duty time together as well, and Wolff knew from the way Mojo was acting tonight, that they were in for another memorable evening. Sure enough, two women, one a blonde and the other a dark haired Hispanic, soon walked up to their table.

"Mind if we join you?" the blonde asked the co-pilot.

"Not at all, ladies," Mugabe said getting to his feet. "I am Jumal Mugabe and this is my friend Rick Wolff."

"I'm Lily," the blonde said. "Pleased to meet you."

"My name's Maria," the dark haired girl said, looking Wolff up and down slowly.

The woman's throaty voice reached down inside Wolff and did strange things to him. He jumped to his feet and pulled a chair out for her. "Do you come here often?" he asked lamely, trying to collect his cool.

"I came here tonight, didn't I?"

While the two chopper cops plied their dates with drinks, Sandra Revell and her Coast Guard officer date were dining in the exclusive Emerald Suite restaurant at the top of the Seattle Space Needle. Built for the 1962 Seattle World's Fair, the spire of the Space Needle with its revolving restaurants on top was a national landmark.

The Coastie wasn't taking any chances with this date and had gone all out. In his experience, the aerial view of Seattle never failed to get a woman in the right frame of mind for a little nightcap in his highrise condo overlooking the harbor. There was something about being so high up in the air that always got the juices flowing. He could hardly wait to see this tall blonde with her juices flowing.

Like any first time visitor, Sandra was fascinated with the Space Needle, but she was not as fascinated with her date. He had seemed to be an interesting man in the bar, but once they were in the restaurant, she felt alone again. Once more, the gulf between being a cop and being a citizen was apparent. Even though this man was a federal officer, he wasn't a police officer and they really didn't have a lot in common.

Sandra's self-imposed rule about not dating the men she worked with was her defense against being taken for just another thrill-seeking bimbo playing around in a man's job. She had worked hard to get where she was and didn't book any crap from anyone about being a woman cop. She had never turned down an assignment, no matter how tough, and she had never complained when the men tried to make her lose her temper or quit. Anytime she got any flak from one of the men, she just waited until the next hand-to-hand class and then kicked his ass up between his ears.

As a result, Sandra Revell was respected as a cop and most of the men she worked with almost seemed to have forgotten that she was a woman. Some of the rest of them, however, stung by her refusal to play silly games, thought that she was a lesbian. She really didn't give a damn what they thought, but she had to admit that her love life hadn't been that great lately. Too many of the men she had dated had figured her for an easy screw just because she was a cop.

This guy she had chosen to go out with tonight was a good case in point. She knew that he was prepping her for a long night in the sack. The fancy restaurant, the expensive wine, the long stories about how important he was, had all been carefully orchestrated to make her fall into his bed at the end of the evening. He actually wasn't a bad guy and he was

55

trying his best, but it wasn't going to work. Not him, not tonight, not ever.

The lieutenant was telling her some story of shipboard intrigue regarding classified documents and she was listening with only half an ear. Looking out in the direction of the harbor, Sandra noticed a chopper flying low over the area of town that the lieutenant had said was called "Little Saigon." From where she was, she couldn't make out what kind of helicopter it was, one of theirs or a local machine, but it took her mind off listening to her date.

She was watching the chopper go into a graceful banking turn when she saw a flash, a blue light laser designator, followed by a streak of fire lancing up from a rooftop. The streak of fire reached the chopper and blossomed into a ball of boiling flame. The shock wave of the explosion rattled the windows, halting the Coast Guard officer's fascinating story.

He spun around in his chair in shock. "My God! What was that?"

"Oh damn!" Sandra breathed softly as the flaming wreckage fell to the street. She pulled the personal communicator from her purse and switched it on.

"Dragon Control," she transmitted, "This is Dragon One Five X-Ray, I am Code Seven at the Space Needle. I just saw a helicopter shot down over downtown Seattle."

"One Five X-Ray, this is Control," came the calm voice of Ruby Jenkins back at the TOC. "Copy. We're getting the information now, it was a Seattle PD chopper, not one of ours. Command One has ordered an immediate recall. How copy?"

"This is One Five X-Ray, copy. I'll be there in fifteen minutes."

The Coast Guard officer was still staring sickly at the fire in the street. "Sorry about this," Sandra said when she could get his attention. "But, duty calls."

Back at the TPF Tactical Operations Center, Buzz Corcran stood behind Ruby Jenkins and monitored the radio traffic from the Seattle PD while a battle raged in the Boa

Hoa controlled section of "Little Saigon." Apparently, a routine police check had triggered a panic response from the gang. When a Seattle PD chopper had responded to a call for assistance, it had been blown out of the sky. More units had responded and they too were now pinned down by heavy gunfire. Obviously, they had come a little too close to something very important.

Corcran wondered if it was something like the missing Trident warhead.

So far, the Seattle cops hadn't called on Dragon Flight for assistance. They were getting their asses kicked down there. They weren't equipped to stand up to that kind of a firefight. A few passes from a pair of the Griffins would get that situation squared away in short order.

"Dragon Control, this is One Zero. When are we going to get permission to take off?"

Buzz keyed his microphone. "One Zero, this is Command One, be advised that we do not have clearance yet. You are to remain on ramp alert till further notice."

"One Zero, copy."

Corcran could hear the disgust in Wolff's voice. He hated sitting on the helipad waiting for something to happen. As always, Wolff and his gunner had been the first to get to their machine when he had sounded the recall. Jennings and Revell in One Five had been hot on their heels. The Griffins were locked and loaded, ready to get out there and kick some ass, but it didn't look like they were going to get a chance to lift off the pad tonight. The mayor of Seattle had still not given his permission for the Tac Force to go into action. And, under the federal law, he had to give his permission before the TPF could operate within his city limits.

Only as long as the Federal Tactical Police Act hadn't been evoked yet, that was.

The law that had created the United States Tactical Police Force in 1996 had also laid down specific ground rules for their employment. The federal government wasn't trying to run roughshod over state and local authorities, but it was an acknowledged fact that crime in many cities had gotten completely out of control. And, in Corcran's experience the local police usually didn't call for federal help until somebody had needlessly been hurt and the time was long past for a quick solution to the problem.

This was turning into one of those times, Corcran could feel it in his bones. The Seattle PD had already lost a chopper, and from what he was hearing on the radio, more cops were pinned down by automatic weapons fire. This fiasco reminded him all too much of some of those monkey fucks he had been a part of during the Vietnam war. At least back then, though, someone would finally get their heads out of the sand and call in a little artillery, an airstrike or something. Here those poor bastards were pitting their police sidearms and shotguns against maggots armed with the Army's latest assault rifles. And, as could be imagined, they were getting their butts kicked. Royally.

Buzz had been a young, hot-rock, Huey gunship pilot with the 1st Air Cav in the Vietnam war and had picked up his nickname when he had made a high speed, low level run over the Division HQ at An Khe after a very successful mission. Unfortunately, he had made his run right over the general's personal latrine and the general had been on his throne when the rotor blast had tipped it over. Corcran had been lucky that he hadn't spent the rest of his tour picking up cigarette butts on the Ho Chi Minh trail.

After two tours in the Cav, and four purple hearts, he had finally decided that he needed a less exciting occupation. He resigned his commission from the Army and went into the helicopter maintenance business in California. After a year of that, though, he was bored out of his mind and answered an ad looking for chopper pilots for the California State Highway Patrol. It turned out that cruising up and down the crowded freeways looking for speeders wasn't exciting enough for him either and he soon joined up as a pilot with the Federal Drug Enforcement Agency.

That had been a real challenge, particularly when the president's war on drugs had heated up. He had led the first contingent of DEA gunships into Colombia and Peru to do battle with the cocaine barons and their private armies. Corcran had been in his element there, fighting drug guerrillas in the jungle.

When the TPF was formed in 1996, he transferred over from the DEA and had been chosen to command the first Dragon Flight. He enjoyed running his unit, but he resented having to be deskbound most of the time. At heart he was still a pilot and each year he somehow managed to wrangle enough hours behind the controls of one of the Griffins to keep his flight status active.

It was times like this, though, that he really resented not being strapped into the cockpit of a gunship, even if it was a gunship on ramp alert that was probably not going anywhere tonight."

"Buzz," Ruby Jenkins asked. "Are you going to report this to Denver too?"

Jenkins was one of the few people who could get away with reminding Corcran of his duties. But then, Mom was a legend in federal law enforcement and could do just about anything that she wanted. Ruby had been one of the first female special agents in the FBI and had made a name for herself on dangerous undercover assignments against terrorist and drug operations.

Her reputation for tackling difficult assignments had been crowned when she had tracked down the assassins who had poisoned California's governor and his anti-war activist wife at the dedication of the Peace Activist Memorial in San Francisco's McArthur park in 1992.

The deaths had been caused by strychnine and Angel-Dust-laden cocaine that had been offered in the "hospitality room" provided by the event's organizers. At first the poisonings had appeared to be accidental, just more bad dope. But Ruby had picked up a rumor that the poisoned cocaine had been placed there by expatriate South African mercenaries working for a radical conservative group.

Ruby had doggedly followed the rumor, tracking the Afrikanners to their operating base in Northern Ireland, but the Irish authorities had refused to extradite them. The South Africans were a valuable part of Northern Ireland's foreign policy arm and they were not about to compromise that over the death of one of their loudest critics.

The unwelcome international publicity that had resulted from that episode, however, had worked against her. While on her next assignment, her cover was blown and she had almost been killed. Reassigned to a boring desk job, Ruby had jumped at the chance to become the operations sergeant for Dragon Flight when the job was offered to her. Now, Buzz commanded Dragon Flight, but she ran operations with an iron fist.

"I think I will give Denver a call," Corcran finally answered. "We've got to invoke the act and get this shit stopped before this whole place goes up in flames."

"Or a mushroom cloud," Ruby added.

"Yeah," Buzz agreed. Even during the crisis of the last few hours, he hadn't forgotten that there was a Trident nuclear missile warhead running around loose out there somewhere. "Patch me in on the scrambler."

CHAPTER 8

"Little Saigon"

Deep in the basement of his "Little Saigon" headquarters, Ex-North Vietnamese Army Colonel Nguyen Cao Dong monitored his police band radio while his men battled the Seattle police outside. With the loss of the men Xuan had left behind in the forest to cover his withdrawal, he had been expecting something like this to happen. It was the only thing that had gone wrong with his carefully laid plan.

Even so, there was almost no chance that the police would cause him any real difficulties tonight. His men would keep them from reaching his headquarters, but this meant that he would have to move the Trident warhead before the nuclear weapons technician was finished with his work.

The missile's eight nuclear MIRVs, the Multiple-targeting Independent Re-entry Vehicles, had to be separated from the main warhead and converted to command detonated bombs before they would be of any use to him. The technician was working as fast as he could on them, but it was delicate work and Dong knew that it could not be rushed. There was nothing to be gained if the MIRVs would not detonate when he wanted them to go off.

He had hoped to have one bomb fused with the radio control unit and ready to be put into place, but it wasn't finished yet. There was nothing to be done now but to move them. That also meant moving the technician and his whores along with the bombs, and that entailed a small risk. He had hoped to be able to keep the man ignorant of the warhead's final destination, but that had to change now. It meant that

61

once the technician had outlived his usefulness, he would have to be eliminated along with his girls.

Recruiting the technician had been easy. This man had once been a missile technician on an U.S. navy missile sub, a Boomer, before his huge gambling debts had brought him to Dong's attention. A place to gamble on credit and a steady supply of young Oriental girls were all the man needed. Both of these were things that Dong could easily supply. His gambling establishments were always open and the young girls came from the poorer Asian refugee families who were always willing to sell their daughters to a rich man, and Dong was wealthy.

Even by American standards, Nguyen Cao Dong was a very rich man.

When the Third Indochinese war had ended in 1975, Dong had been a young officer with the invading North Vietnamese Army that had swept into the old southern capital of Saigon. Even though the conquerors quickly renamed it Ho Chi Minh City, the character of Saigon did not change. There was still plenty of money to be made by a man who didn't mind catering to human vices, and vices were something that Dong knew well.

In the early days of the NVA occupation, Dong was in charge of the squads that searched the conquered city for enemies of the state who were to be apprehended and brought to justice at the hands of the People's Courts. Dong was good at his job, his men rounded up hundreds of men and women for the re-education camps. But, very early on, he discovered that there were two kinds of enemies of the state, those who were wealthy and those who were not.

The first time that Dong was offered a substantial bribe to look the other way while someone escaped, he had been shocked. Not at being offered a bribe, but at the size of the bribe, more money than he could expect to make in ten years. He not only took the offered money, but required that the would-be refugee to add even more money to the pot to insure that the other squads looking for the man would not find him. Dong knew when he had found a good thing.

Suddenly, Dong found himself a rich man, a very rich

man, by Communist standards. However, with a canny insight to the minds of his Communist masters, he was careful to make no display of his new wealth. When he captured one of old Saigon's more famous brothel keepers, however, he did invest some of his money in a new enterprise, the best whorehouse in Saigon.

Not only did Dong provide women in his establishment, he also tapped into the old black market sources of western liquor and, once he discovered that there was a demand for it, the age old Golden Triangle drug trading networks. Soon, the money he was making from fleecing refugees became a drop in the bucket compared to what he was making from his other business enterprises.

Soon, Dong branched out even further. He learned that many of his clients preferred their entertainment to be a little more exotic than his usual fare. Particularly, entertainment considerably younger than the ones he usually offered. Since he was still the officer in charge of an enemies of the state unit, Dong switched from taking bribes in gold to taking them in human flesh. The young sons and daughters of would-be refugees soon found themselves working in Dong's establishment.

This became Dong's high road to power. Visiting high ranking Communists from the rigid, puritanical North found every excuse possible to visit Ho Chi Minh City so they could sample Dong's wares. Dong, ever wise to the ways of power, made gifts of young prostitutes, both boys and girls, and drugs to those in power. They in turn saw that Dong rose quickly in the Communist hierarchy and he soon became the youngest lieutenant colonel in the North Vietnamese Army.

This situation might have lasted forever had not an unfortunate incident occurred.

Dong's meteoric rise to power had not been without a certain risk. Even though many of Dong's clients were among the highest of the People's Republic of Vietnam's leaders, there were others in power who clung to the old puritanical ethics of Asian Marxism and detested Dong as a corrupting, reactionary influence. Due to Dong's protectors in high places, however, they were powerless to move against him until the night that the son of Hanoi's minister of defense visited Dong's establishment.

This young man, a major in the North Vietnamese secret service, had secret yearnings that he had not been able to fully satisfy in Hanoi. Yearnings for the thrills of young flesh experienced through the heightened awareness brought on only by the use of certain drugs. Unfortunately, the major had not been used to the purity of Dong's drugs and had died with his hands around the neck of the young girl who had been servicing him. Also, the young major's personal bodyguard had been in attendance when this unfortunate incident occurred and they accused Dong of having poisoned their major.

Dong had always known that there was a possibility that his services to his country would suddenly come to an end one day and he had prepared for that eventuality.

When Dong fled Vietnam that night in his oceangoing yacht, he carried several million dollars worth of high quality gem stones, mostly diamonds, with him. He was immediately able to go back into business in America, the Land of Golden Opportunity.

Dong quickly re-established his old drug contacts and the flow of Asian heroin and hashish began anew. Once the drug pipe line was in place, the rest came quite easily. He quickly built another private army every bit as effective as the Vietnamese enemies of the state unit he had commanded before, the Boa Hoa. There was no shortage of men who would follow a leader such as Dong. Most of his men were Vietnamese, but he recruited from the other Asian communities as well to spread his powerbase.

Taking a page from the American Mafia's operating manual, Dong soon had a hand in almost everything that happened in "Little Saigon." His men collected taxes from businessmen, sold permits for everything from opening a shop to renting an apartment. Trucks paid a toll to insure that they were not hijacked from the back streets when they made their deliveries. Whenever there was resistance to Dong's shadow government, another mutilated body would be found in the harbor. Soon, there was no resistance.

As the years passed, however, Dong became dissatisfied with his private kingdom. Controlling Seattle's "Little Saigon" was not enough for him and he opened contacts with the governments of both Red China and North Korea as a road to bigger operations.

At first he had simply supplied these governments with top secret hi-tech information and equipment smuggled past U.S. customs agents. And, once he had proven himself to his Communist allies, plans were made that would satisfy the hunger of any megalomaniac. The Trident warhead he had stolen would finally give him the means to satisfy his cravings. But, preparing the warhead for the planned operation was being threatened by the battle raging outside. Something had to be done to get the police off his back while he moved his stolen prize to his island.

Dong turned to one of the men in the room. "Tell Xuan to start moving the warhead operation to the island immediately," he ordered.

"As you command, sir."

"Also, send the captain of the Red Fist Commando in to see me immediately."

The Red Fist Commando was a special unit of terrorists he had formed as part of his bigger plans. Trained in North Korea, these men would be the fist that would hammer out his new empire.

"You asked to see me, sir?"

Dong looked up to see a stocky, young Vietnamese dressed in camouflague fatigues and a red beret standing at a rigid position of attention. Tri Quan Minh was one of the best of his men, a man who would rise to a high position once the missile warhead had done its job.

"Yes, Captain Minh. Two things, first the commandos who were captured today are to be killed without delay. This time there can be no excuses, they must be killed before they can talk."

Minh knew that those men were being held in the downtown TPF field office and it would be almost impossible to get to them, but he didn't even blink. If Colonel Dong wanted them dead, they would die. "At your command!" he replied, his face blank.

"Secondly," Dong continued. "The police are interfering with my plans, so I want the Space Needle takeover put into operation tomorrow."

That particular part of the overall operation had been planned to take place in two days, but again, Minh didn't even blink. "At your command!"

"You are dismissed."

Minh saluted, sharply spun around on his heels and marched out.

Nguyen Cao Dong, once colonel of the North Vietnamese Army and vice lord of Ho Chi Minh City, smiled as the door shut behind him. That should get the long noses off his back for awhile. Quite awhile.

Back at the TPF TOC, Buzz Corcran waited impatiently for Denver to call back and give him permission to invoke the Tactical Police Force Act, turning control of all police operations in the Greater Seattle area to Dragon Flight. As always, it was taking a long time to get the necessary political clearance. Even when there was a stolen nuclear warhead involved, it still took far too long for someone to make a decision. It was so typical of the bureaucratic bungling that came with belonging to a federal agency.

While he was waiting, he turned to Ruby. "Put the word out that there will be a briefing at zero eight hundred tomorrow," he said.

"Yes, sir," she answered.

"They should have gotten off their hands in Washington by then," Buzz growled. "And we can start getting this rotten mess under control."

Ruby didn't bother to reply; she knew that Buzz was just talking to himself again. He did that a lot recently, particularly when the powers that be didn't see things his way or move fast enough to suit him. She had been around Buzz long enough to know that he would be growling like a bear with a wounded paw until this whole thing was wrapped up and there was no point in even noticing it.

She switched to the all channel mode and keyed her throat mike.

"All stations," she radioed. "This is Dragon Control, be advised that there will be a command group briefing at . . ."

CHAPTER 9

TPF Tactical Operations Center

Five minutes before it was scheduled to start, every man and woman of Dragon Flight was in the Coast Guard conference room that had been borrowed for the briefing. By now, everyone knew about the missing nuclear weapons and the gang battle that had occurred the night before. Bad news travels fast in a police force.

At precisely eight o'clock, Captain Buzz Corcran entered the room followed by a man in civilian clothes and an older uniformed police officer. Corcran looked grim as he briskly strode up to the podium. "This is Mister Johnson," he announced. "The mayor of Greater Seattle and Captain Williams, the chief of police. They're going to sit in on our briefing today."

The Tac Force commander was immaculately dressed in his TPF Class A Blues, his silver Army pilot's wings gleaming above his TPF gold wings and his military service ribbons. Both the mayor and the chief, however, looked rumpled and red-eyed as if they had been up all night. The two men took seats in the front row.

"First," Corcran continued, looking directly at the two outsiders. "I want to remind you that the contents of this briefing fall under the Official Secrets Act and are not to be revealed to anyone without prior clearance. Now, Lieutenant Tran of the Seattle field office will give us a background briefing."

The Vietnamese-American walked to the front of the room and faced his audience. "As most of you have heard," he started, "we have a particularly dangerous situation here. At

68

approximately ten hundred hours yesterday, the warhead of a Trident II missile was stolen from a hijacked train. According to the Nuclear Weapons Commission, that warhead contains eight separate 20 kiloton nuclear weapons, any one of which could destroy most of Seattle. We have good reason to believe that those weapons are in the hands of a local Vietnamese gang that call themselves the Boa Hoa."

Tran saw no need to go into details about the fact that the two prisoners from the train hijacking had identified themselves only in the short time they had been in custody. They had been fed poison with their breakfasts and would reveal nothing further now. The Asian cook who had administered the poison had disappeared shortly thereafter and was currently being sought.

"This organization is headed by an ex-colonel of the North Vietnamese Army who is a complete lunatic, Nguyen Cao Dong."

No one in the audience thought it strange that Tran had used the term "North Vietnamese" instead of the Democratic Republic of Vietnam as it had been called since the northern Communists had overrun the south in 1975. As a son of South Vietnamese refugees, Tran would always think of his country as being divided into North and South Vietnam.

The lights automatically dimmed as a life-sized holograph appeared to the side of the stage. The holo showed a small, thin Oriental man with a sharp face, dark hair and deep, almost black eyes. The computer generating the holo made the figure face to both the right and the left as if he were in a police lineup. There was nothing particularly striking about Dong until you looked at the eyes. Tran was right, they were the burning eyes of a true fanatic.

"We have known about Dong's gang for quite some time, but until recently, he hasn't been a serious problem. As with most of the Asian gangs on the West Coast, the Boa Hoa has worked the drug trade with a little extortion, gambling, and prostitution on the side. For the most part, their activities have been confined to the large Asian community in Seattle, particularly the Vietnamese population in 'Little Saigon' where his influence is strongest."

Tran killed the holo and consulted his notes. "In the last year, however, Dong has been expanding his operations into the non-Asian community. In the process, he has come up against other established crime organizations and the battle in 'Little Saigon' last night is not the first time that violence has resulted. All of that, however, pales compared to the fact that Dong now has his hands on the missing warhead. Additionally, we have confirmed that his people also have advanced Army infantry weapons from the hijacked shipment that Dragon Flight was sent up here to locate.

"What we're looking at here is an extremely dangerous situation. We are facing a well-armed opponent who has no compunction whatsoever against using armed force. The only thing we don't know is what he intends to do with those nukes. But, whatever it is, we have to recover them before Seattle, or somewhere else for that matter, gets blown away in a nuclear firestorm."

When Tran took his seat, Corcran stepped back up to the podium. "Briefing packets are being handed out that summarizes the information that we now have on ex-Colonel Dong and his gang. It also gives the specifications on the Army weapons that we now know he has armed his people with. I expect everyone to go over this material at their first opportunity and keep it in mind during this operation. We aren't going up against a bunch of mentals armed with the typical AK-47, M-16 or Uzi gang weapons. These people are using the Army's latest weaponry, M-25 assault rifles, Scorpion anti-tank rocket launchers and Viper anti-aircraft missiles."

The captain scanned the rows of officers in the conference room. "You pilots and aircrew officers had better read the details about that Viper very carefully. When you've memorized them, talk to Sergeant Wolff and Officer Mugabe about their run-in with it. Unfortunately, you can't talk to the pilots of the King County and Seattle police choppers who came into contact with the Viper; they're dead."

Corcran sorted through his briefing material for a moment. "Okay, here's the drill for now. First thing, the missing nukes. Until we can develop some hard intelligence about them, there's very little that we can do. Lieutenant Tran has his people out on the street right now trying to sniff out anything they can about them. Also, Denver headquarters is sending us a team of experts to install special neutrino emissions sensor equipment in our Griffins that should allow us to detect the nukes from the air."

Corcran looked up from his notes. "Until they get here, however, we have another item on the agenda—putting an end to the gang problem in downtown Seattle."

Corcran looked over at the Seattle police chief sitting in the front row. "Captain Williams, would you care to brief us on that situation?"

Williams got to his feet and walked behind the podium. He looked like a man who had been pushed to the limits of his endurance. "As you all know, four Seattle police officers were killed in last night's battle in "Little Saigon" when their helicopter was shot out of the sky. Three more officers were wounded in the street fighting and one of them is not expected to live."

He paused for a moment as if to collect his thoughts. "We have had gun battles with the gangs in that area before, but never anything like this. This was open warfare and we got hurt badly."

The police chief straightened himself and his voice hardened. "The Seattle police department has to get this situation under control as quickly as we can and I have asked the Tactical Police Force to give us a hand with this operation."

The chief's words brought the mayor bolt upright in his chair. "You can't do that," he sputtered. "This is a local problem and we can . . ."

"Mayor," Corcran cut him off. "As of twenty-four hundred hours last night, the Greater Seattle area has been declared a Federal Criminal Emergency Area under the provisions of the Tactical Police Force Act of 1996. The Tac Force is now in control of all police activities in your city and the surrounding area."

The mayor leaped to his feet, his face flushed. "But, you can't do that," he shouted. "No one said anything to me . . ."

"Mister Mayor," Corcran said again. "This is out of your hands now. You might as well go back to City Hall and prepare a statement for the press. They'll pick up on this fast enough and your people had better have some answers to their questions." Mayor Johnson got to his feet and slowly walked out. As soon as the mayor closed the door behind him, Corcran scanned the officers sitting in front of him. "Wolff?"

"Yo!" The pilot answered from the back of the room.

"I want you and Mojo to fly C and C for this operation."

"Yes, sir," Wolff answered with a big grin on his face. "How many ships are we using?"

"I want everybody in the air for this one," the captain said. "I doubt that we'll have targets for all four ships, but I want to intimidate the hell out of these people. I don't want them to look up without seeing a Griffin hovering right over their heads."

"Can do, sir," The Wolfman answered.

"As for the rest of you," Corcran continued. "I want the Air-Ground Operations people to mount up and move out with the heavies this time."

Lieutenant Ramón de Avila, the Air Ground Coordinator, nodded as he took notes. His operation could be mounted in a modified Army M-2 Bradley tracked vehicle, so they could be right on the scene when the Griffins went into action.

"Medical support," Corcran continued. "Will be provided by Seattle's hospitals and ambulance services. Fire stations will be notified of the operation and will be on call."

Corcran looked up from his notes and paused. "Rules of Engagement Charlie are in effect for the duration of this operation."

A muted murmur came from the Tac Force officers in the room. The TPF had three levels of deadly force governed by the Alpha, Bravo and Charlie Rules of Engagement. ROE Alpha only allowed the use of weapons to save a life, Bravo allowed the Tac Cops to shoot back at anyone who shot at them and Charlie was a shoot on sight order and was rarely authorized. The fact that Washington had authorized ROE Charlie meant that they were taking the situation seriously. Very seriously.

Under Rules of Engagement Charlie, anyone seen packing a weapon or committing a crime was dead meat. The Tac Force cops wouldn't have to wait to be shot at first this time.

"Excellent!" someone said out loud.

Corcran looked up to find the outspoken cop. "This does not mean, however, that you hot dogs don't have to use a little common sense," he cautioned. "I don't want any little old ladies getting wasted because some clown thought they saw her packing a piece."

Corcran turned on the projector and a map of downtown Seattle appeared on the screen. "We're going to kick this off tonight at eighteen hundred hours from these four positions." The captain used a light wand to pinpoint the starting points.

"The Seattle PD is providing most of the ground troops including their SWAT teams, but we are getting two heavy patrol cars to carry the Tactical Platoon as well as sending in the Griffins."

The TPF heavy patrol cars were six-wheeled armored cars capable of carrying ten fully-armed Tac Platoon officers in the compartment in back. They were fitted with a turret that could be armed with a variety of weapons and their armor would withstand hits up to fifty caliber armor-piercing rounds. Like the Griffin choppers, the heavies were the latest thing in police hardware.

"We'll wrap this thing up when it's finished," Corcran warned. "So don't plan any hot dates, you're going to be busy most of the night." He looked around at the men and women in the room. "Any questions?"

There were none.

"Okay," Buzz scanned the room. "Zumwald, I want to see you in my office. The rest of you are dismissed until seventeen hundred tonight."

As the rest of Dragon Flight filed out of the briefing room, TPF Lieutenant Jack Zumwald, leader of the Tactical Platoon, followed his commander into his office.

The hall outside the briefing room was buzzing as the meeting broke up. Wolff and Mugabe pushed their way through the crowd trying to make it to the door when someone shouted, "Hey, Wolfman!"

Wolff turned to see Ramon de Avila, the Air-Ground Ops officer, waving at him. "I need to talk to you about something," he yelled over the crowd.

Wolff pointed to the door and continued on his way. Outside, he and Mugabe waited till the slender Hispanic officer could join them. "Look," he said, "I've got an idea about those Vipers."

"Lay it on me, Lieutenant," Mugabe said.

"Put one of your birds in high orbit over the operational area with all her sensors looking for the first sign of a missile laser designator. I'll be tac linked to him and shooting the data to the rest of you guys. That way, you can go on about your business. If the high man spots a missile, you'll get the lock-on signal instantly and can duck for cover without having to look around to see where the launcher is. I can get his location from the high man's tac link and vector you into him."

"How about the poor bastard flying high cover for us?" Wolff asked. "The guy with the Viper is going to figure out what he's doing and tear him to pieces. That high up, he won't have a place a hide and if his mirror skin can't break the lock-on, he'll be dead meat."

Avila thought for a moment. "Shit! I was hoping to find some way to make this a little easier for you guys."

"I think the best thing," Mugabe said. "Is for us all to stay down low, down around the roof tops. Tac link everybody together and tie into your computer map. You can handle six channels at once, can't you?"

Avila nodded.

"That way," Mugabe continued, "we can still break on the first lock-on signal and you can try to locate him for us."

"Sounds good," Avila shrugged. "I'll pass the word. Those gang bastards got no chance."

"Yeah," Wolff said, putting on his aviator shades, "if we get lucky."

CHAPTER 10

Downtown Seattle

While the men and women of Dragon Flight started preparing for the evening's operation, Lieutenant Tran went back to his office in the Federal Building and quickly changed into civilian clothing. That screwup with the prisoners this morning had left him without a single lead to the missing warhead. He had all of his people out on the street already, hitting every contact they had, but Tran was afraid that it was not going to work fast enough. He had a couple of personal contacts that only he could talk to, and to do that, he had to hit the bricks himself in plain clothes.

As soon as he was dressed, he checked the load in the magazine of his 10mm Glock pistol and holstered it under his left arm inside his Nike wind breaker. The jacket was loose enough that the weapon would not show if he kept the zipper caught at the bottom. He usually went unarmed on his trips to "Little Saigon," but things were unsettled enough there now that he wanted the added assurance of the powerful pistol. He did not clip his personal communicator to his belt, however. Where he was going today, it would be a dead giveaway that he was a cop.

"I'm going to be out of contact for a few hours," he told the desk sergeant in the outer office. "I'll be back at about two or three."

"Right, sir," the sergeant said. "If anyone calls, where do you want me to say that you've gone?"

"I'm going to visit some of my relatives."

"Yes, sir."

The Federal Building was only a few blocks from the part of the city that was now known as "Little Saigon." At one time, it had been a chic, tourist area full of overpriced antique shops and boutiques known as Pioneer Square. By the mid-nineties, however, it had been abandoned by the trendy and quickly slid downhill, becoming a haven for drug users and prostitutes as soon as the sun went down.

When the last wave of Southeast Asian boat people had started pouring into Seattle, they had settled the area and had quickly replaced the antique shops with small Asian stores, Oriental restaurants and tea shops. The refugees had been so successful at their enterprises that the Asian population had spread and now populated most of the older part of town from the harbor to Kingdome stadium.

The first block facing the rest of the town presented a colorful Oriental facade, and was accessible to the public. One block into "Little Saigon," however, was a crowded rat's warren of leanto's, small stalls, tables on the sidewalk and looked like any back alley in any crowded Asian city. Tourists rarely went too far into the area.

Quite a few of Tran's relatives still lived in "Little Saigon" and he had spent many boyhood hours on its crowded back streets when he had visited his aunts and uncles. He still spent many hours there, but like today, most of his visits now were strictly business.

Sitting down at a sidewalk table in front of a tiny Vietnamese soup shop, he lit up a New Salem cigarette. Tran normally didn't smoke, but the cigarette was camouflage as were the black pants and white shirt he wore with the gaudy windbreaker. To an outsider, he would look like any of a dozen other Asians passing time sitting at one of the dozen similar, small establishments lining the block.

The waiter, an older man, quickly approached. *"Chao ong,"* he greeted Tran politely.

"Chao ong, Ba Moui Ba," he answered, ordering the French beer once very popular with the millions of American GIs in Southeast Asia.

The waiter quickly returned and glanced up and down the street as he set a glass in front of the cop and poured the beer.

76

"It is dangerous for you to be seen here," he told Tran in Vietnamese.

Tran slowly took a drink. "And why is that?" he asked quietly.

"They know who you are," the old man answered. The waiter didn't have to explain who "they" were, Tran knew that the man referred to the Boa Hoa. "They are showing many pictures of you to the cowboys and they are offering a big reward for your death."

"Cowboy" was the Vietnamese nickname for the petty gangsters that plagued every Asian refugee community. Usually younger than the full-fledged gang members, the cowboys served as runners and auxiliaries for the Boa Hoa and the tongs. If they did well with their youthful assignments, they would be rewarded by being accepted into the ranks of the gangs. Having cowboys after him could be a greater danger than the Boa Hoa, but Tran shrugged off the threat.

"They have known who I am for a long time," Tran replied. "Why do they want me dead now?"

"I do not know."

"What else are you hearing?" the cop asked.

The old man paused. "Something important is happening," he said slowly. "But they fall silent when I bring them their drinks, so I hear nothing." He thought for a moment, "Also, I see many of the young men smile secretly."

"Do you know what started that gunfire with the police last night?"

The waiter shrugged, "I did not see what happened, but I heard that officers from a patrol car tried to catch one of the Boa Hoa. They chased him into a building and were ambushed."

"And the helicopter?"

The waiter shrugged. "I know nothing about that, just that it crashed."

"What was in that building that is so important?"

"Only one of Colonel Dong's gambling parlors."

"Have you seen any unusual truck traffic in that area?"

The old man paused to think. "No, just the regular delivery trucks."

Tran thought for a moment. Dong had never been known to defend one of his establishments with that kind of firepower before. Maybe there was something else going on in there other than a crooked, high stakes poker game. Something that he would like to know about, such as a missing missile warhead. Maybe this was the lead he needed.

He drained the last of his beer and slid his chair back. Laying a folded bill under his glass, he got to his feet. *"Chao ong,"* he said goodbye to the waiter.

"Chao ong." The waiter bowed slightly and slid his hand over the bill.

Tran lit up another Salem and walked around the corner to the site of last night's gunfight. He had read the Seattle PD after-action report of the battle, but he wanted to take a good look at the area himself. The gambling hall was scheduled for a thorough search in tonight's sweep, but it wouldn't hurt to recon it first to get an idea of the layout inside. Maybe he'd even stop off at one of the tables and play a few hands of cards. Maybe he'd even get lucky and win back the fifty dollars he had paid the old man for his information.

Tran knew that he was taking a big risk going in there alone. But he was anxious to get some lead on the missing nuke and was counting on Dong's men not expecting a well-known federal cop to walk into one of his strongholds.

The wreckage of the Seattle PD chopper had been removed from the intersection, but melted asphalt and smoke stains showed where it had crashed. Fortunately, it had fallen on the street and not into one of the crowded apartment buildings that lined the block. As it was, no one had been killed except the Seattle cops.

Dong's building took up most of the block, a large, turn-of-the-century, three-story brick structure that had been converted into shops and apartments. The ground floor housed an Oriental restaurant, a camera shop, a garage and a small grocery store, all legitimate businesses. A stairwell at the end of the building led up to the apartments on the second floor. The apartments were legitimate too, a screen for the activities on the third floor.

As Tran walked down the long hall between the apartments, the odors of Oriental cooking wafting through the air brought back memories of a childhood spent in a building very much like this one.

At the end of the corridor, a modern steel fire door closed off another stairwell. From the weight of the door when he opened it, Tran knew that it was armored. Without being too obvious about it, he noted the massive remote-controlled electronic lock, the same kind that was used to lock jail cells. He looked for a video camera head, but didn't see one. That didn't mean that the door wasn't under observation, however. Micro cameras no bigger than the head of a nail could be hidden anywhere along the hall leading up to the door. He was walking into a trap that could be snapped shut behind him at any moment and he felt a tingle run down his back.

The federal cop almost turned and went back. He knew that he was getting in well over his head and should simply take what he had learned and run. He continued on up the stairs, however. He had come this far and wanted to see the rest of this urban fortress. At the top of the stairs was a bright red, ornately carved wooden door. At least it looked like wood. It could have been bullet proof, molded Lexan plastic for all he knew. A buzzer was set into the wall at the side of the door frame and he pressed the button.

Again, he could not see any video camera heads, but he had a tingling sensation that he was being watched. The red door unlocked with a buzz and opened a few inches. He pushed it the rest of the way open and walked into a dimly lit, short hallway. As soon as Tran's eyes adjusted to the light, he knew that he'd hit the jackpot. He also knew that he had just stepped in deep shit when he heard the door click shut behind him.

A guard with a semi-automatic pistol sat at a small, round table and the muzzle of the pistol was aimed squarely at Tran's chest. The second man standing behind the guard was Le Duc Xuan, Dong's second-in-command, and Xuan knew him well. They had grown up on the crowded streets of "Little Saigon" together.

Xuan smiled slowly as he brought up his own pistol. "Raise your hands slowly," he said quietly.

Tran quickly did as he was told. The guard easily discovered the Glock 10mm in the shoulder holster and relieved him of it. "Turn around and put your hands behind your back," Xuan commanded.

Again Tran did not resist as the guard quickly slipped a plastic restraint over the cop's wrists, snugged it down tight and turned him around again.

"It was very foolish for you to come here, Phan Le Tran," Xuan said.

Tran had no choice but to agree.

High in the Emerald Suite at the top of the Space Needle overlooking the city below, Mayor Johnson sat down to thundering applause. His speech about the bright economic future of Seattle had been well received by the delegates of the 5th Pacific Rim Economic Summit Conference. He had been a little concerned that the battle in "Little Saigon" last night might have put his administration and the city in a bad light. Actually, though, the operation had turned out to be a plus for his reputation as a civic leader.

Right after the TPF briefing, his media "advisor" had held a quick news conference that had turned a potential catastrophe into a visionary crusade to keep the criminal element from taking over a large part of town. No mention had been made of the losses the Seattle police department had suffered and nothing had been said about the upcoming TPF sweep of the area tonight. He'd explain away those bothersome little details when he had to.

Fortunately, the delegates from the Pacific Rim countries also saw the incident that way. They were used to their own police forces cleaning up their cities when dignitaries were due to visit and saw nothing unusual about the operation.

The mayor looked out over the edge of the Space Needle at the city more than five hundred feet below. He was glad that he had let himself be talked into holding the opening luncheon in the newly remodeled Emerald Suite of the famous monument. Initially, he had wanted to hold it in the newly remodeled civic auditorium, but Mai Lin, his Vietnamese born Asian public relations advisor, had argued that the delegates would be more impressed with the Space Needle. Her persuasion had been most convincing, but then he was always convinced when Mai locked her lips on his.

Actually, Johnson probably would have agreed to using the Space Needle even without Mai Lin's special persuasive talents. Being a native Seattleite, he had been around the Space Needle all his life and its novelty had worn off long ago. But he was still aware that it was one of the nation's most dramatic landmarks.

Built as the centerpiece for the 1962 World's Fair, the Space Needle towered 605 feet above the old fairgrounds. Three elevators took visitors to and from the two restaurants and observation deck at the 520 foot level. The entire top of the Space Needle rotated at a rate of one complete turn every hour and gave visitors a fantastic panoramic view of The Puget Sound, the city below and the mountains to the east.

When the World's Fair had ended, seventy-four acres of the fairgrounds had been turned into Seattle's cultural center and was the home to several museums, the Art Pavilion and the famous Space Needle. There were two different restaurants in the flying saucer-like top of the Needle. One was the Space Needle Restaurant and the second the luxurious Emerald Suite where the economic conference was having lunch.

The Space Needle was still a symbol of the 21st Century and it was fitting that the men who would guide the financial destinies of the Pacific Rim into the new millennium were meeting there today.

Johnson glanced down at his watch; they were running a little behind schedule today, but that was not unusual for these things. The representative from South Korea was just finishing his long opening speech and the waiters were standing by to serve lunch. In honor of the delegates, lunch was to be an Oriental feast served by waiters from Seattle's Asian community. Again, Mai Lin had suggested this touch and had made all the arrangements. In more than one way, the mayor didn't know what he would do without that woman.

The South Korean also sat down to thundering applause

and the mayor stepped back up behind the podium. Glancing to the rear of the room, he saw that Mai's waiters were standing by ready to begin serving the meal.

"And now," he said. "We want you to all sit back and enjoy some of the best food from the entire Pacific Northwest. Chefs from Seattle's finest Oriental restaurants have joined together to bring you . . ."

The delegates couldn't help but notice the look of shock on the mayor's face and turned in unison to see what was wrong. The South Korean delegate leaped to his feet, his hand reaching under his jacket at the same time, but he didn't have a chance to bring his pistol to bear. One of the waiters swung the muzzle of an assault rifle around and cut him down with a short burst. The Korean fell back and complete pandemonium broke out.

"No one make a move!" someone shouted over the commotion. "Sit down or you will all die!" The man triggered off a burst of fire into the roof and the room fell silent.

One of the waiters shucked his black coat and tie and ripped off his white shirt. Under his waiter's uniform, he wore camouflaged fatigues. Pulling a red beret from a side pocket, he slapped it on his head.

"You are prisoners of the Red Fist Commando," he proudly announced. "If our demands are met, no one will be harmed. If they are not," he shrugged. "You will all die."

CHAPTER 11

Captain Corcran was still going over the street plans of "Little Saigon" with Lieutenant Zumwald when the intercom on his desk came to life. "Captain," Ruby called. "I think you'd better get in here."

Buzz slid back his chair and headed for the door. Any time that Ruby called him captain, something serious was going down. "What's wrong?" he asked, rounding the corner to the dispatch center.

"Listen to this," she said, flicking a switch on her commo console. A young woman's voice came over the loud-speaker. ". . . and, if our demands are not met by three o'clock this afternoon, we will start killing our hostages at a rate of one an hour until they are all dead. As soon as you are prepared to meet our demands, we can be contacted on this frequency. Red Fist Commando, out."

"Now what the hell is going on?" Buzz exploded.

Mom pushed the button on the tape recorder and played back the tape of the entire radio transmission. All radio and video communications coming into the TOC were automatically recorded in case of a situation like this.

"Attention Seattle Police," the woman's voice said. "This is the Red Fist Commando. We are holding the capitalist delegates to the Pacific Rim Economic Conference hostage in the top of the Space Needle. If you want to see them alive again you will listen very carefully. First, we want . . ."

Buzz listened grimfaced as the woman read a long list of

83

demands. They wanted money, of course, fifty million American dollars, the release of a lengthy list of Asian criminals and terrorists held in federal prisons, safe conduct to a neutral nation and all the rest of the typical demands in a hostage situation. They also vowed that if any action whatsoever was taken against them, they would start killing the hostages immediately.

"Slap a lid on this, now," Buzz commanded when the tape ended. Under the Federal Tactical Police Force Act, he could impose a complete news blackout on any hostage or terrorist incident if he felt that it was necessary to protect lives.

"It's too late," Mom shook her head. "They broadcast their message on channel one, the Seattle police frequency, and the TV stations monitor that channel all the time. We've probably got all four networks on their way to the Space Needle with their mobile units right now."

"Shit!" Buzz reached for the microphone. This was the last thing he needed right now, a damned hostage crisis on top of everything else. "Put me through to Chief Williams downtown ASAP."

He paused for a moment. "And get One Zero in the air," he told Mom. "Tell 'em to stay out of range, but I want someone up there to keep an eye on this thing for me."

"Right away."

As he waited for the Seattle police chief to come on the line, Buzz realized that he had just run out of time to find the stolen warhead before it was reported in the headline news. The Tac Force would break up the hostage situation, there was no question about that in his mind. But when they did, someone was bound to ask what in the hell the nation's elite police force was doing in Seattle in the first place. He could always use their original mission to try to explain that. But all it would take would be for one railroad employee to whisper something about the hijacked White Train and it would all be over but the shouting.

"This is Chief Williams," the deep voice in the com

unit said.

"Captain Corcran," Buzz replied. "First, I want your people to isolate the area around the Space Needle immediately. Evacuate everyone within small arms range of the damned thing. Secondly, I want the hospitals alerted and medical people standing by behind the police barricades. Next, I want a list of everyone attending that damned conference and everyone who works in the Space Needle. And last, I need a set of plans to that thing and I need them yesterday. Any questions?"

"No, sir," the Seattle police chief answered.

"Good. If you have any problems, get to me fast and I mean fast."

He turned to the Tac Platoon leader who had been patiently standing by. Lieutenant Jack Zumwald, Zoomie to his friends, had a big silly grin on his face. He loved this kind of mission. This was a great opportunity for his men to use the new hostage situation drills they had practiced over and over for months on end.

"Zoomie," Buzz said. "Tell your sergeant to get your people suited up and have them stand by."

"Yes, sir."

"And, when you're done with that, get back here so we can plan how in the hell we're going to get those people out of there."

"I'll be back in five."

Buzz took a quick look around the TOC. "Put me through to the field office, I want to talk to Tran," he ordered next.

While Ruby placed the call, Buzz went over to the big topographic map of Greater Seattle and studied the Seattle Center where the Space Needle was located. It was the most ideal place to hold hostages that he could think of. Rising over six hundred feet above the seventy-four acre Seattle Center complex, the only way the tower could be approached was from the air. And even a blind man could see the choppers coming from up there.

No matter how he worked it, there was going to be a gun battle this time and he was afraid that it was going to get real bloody before it was all over.

"Buzz," Ruby said. "The field office is not in contact with Lieutenant Tran."

"Why not, for Christ's sakes?" Buzz exploded. "Isn't his communicator working?"

"He doesn't have it with him."

"Damn!" Buzz reached for the handset. "Let me talk to his operations sergeant then."

"Sergeant Sunami," the voice on the other end of the line said. "Maybe I can help you, sir."

"This is Captain Corcran. First, just who in the hell are the Red Fist Commandos?"

"We've never heard of them, sir," the sergeant said. "They're totally new to us."

"Great!" Buzz was getting madder by the minute. "And just where the hell is your commander?"

"We don't know, sir," the sergeant answered. "He told the desk sergeant that he was going down to 'Little Saigon' to talk to some of his personal contacts and that he expected to be back by two or three."

"Get your people out there," Corcran commanded. "Find him and get him over here ASAP."

"Yes, sir."

Buzz reached up absentmindedly to pat his empty shirt pocket again. This situation was rapidly turning into a world class rat fuck.

Back in Dong's building, Xuan led Tran around the corner of the hall to an elevator. Taking a magnetically coded security card from his pocket, he unlocked the door and motioned the cop inside. Shielding the control panel from Tran's view, Xuan slipped his card into a slot and pushed a button. The elevator silently started downward.

When Xuan moved out of the way, Tran could see that

there were no numbers on the buttons of the control panel, but there were five buttons. Since there were only three floors above ground, the other two buttons had to be for unseen basement floors. From the time that the elevator took to make its descent, Tran could tell that they had gone all the way to the bottom floor.

The door opened to a brightly lit, modern office full of people. Girls in colorful silk ao dais, the Vietnamese national dress, sat behind computer keyboards and answered phones. Others were packing files into cardboard boxes and running papers through a shredder. No one was in a panic, but everyone was working as quickly as they could. It was obvious that Dong was moving his operation.

The guard led Tran through the office to a door at the far end of the room. Xuan knocked lightly and a voice inside speaking Vietnamese ordered them to enter. The guard immediately opened the door and shoved Tran into a lavishly furnished room. The walls were covered with carved wooden panels and ancient Chinese art prints. The floor was carpeted with priceless Oriental rugs. The man sitting behind the ornately carved wooden desk at the end of the room was thin with a sharp face, a face that Tran knew well.

"Colonel Dong, I presume," he said in English.

Dong studied him for a moment, his deep set eyes seeming to burn into him. "You have made a grave mistake by coming here, Lieutenant," he answered in Vietnamese.

Tran shrugged. "I just wanted to play a couple hands of cards upstairs," he said with a big smile, trying to brazen it out.

Dong stared at him for a long moment. "I do not think it is that simple, Lieutenant," the colonel finally said. "You are looking for a missing nuclear missile warhead."

Tran just shrugged his shoulders. There was no point in playing dumb and asking what missing nuclear missile. Dong wasn't stupid. He obviously knew that the Tac Force was on to him or he wouldn't be preparing to abandon his

87

headquarters.

"What do you want me to do with him?" Xuan asked his leader.

Dong thought for a moment. If he killed this federal cop, it might cause him a little more trouble than he had time to deal with right now. He knew how the Tac Force reacted when one of their officers was killed. Right now, the schedule for the operation didn't include any time to waste hiding from a vengeful Tactical Police Force.

He also couldn't afford to just turn Tran loose, even though the building would be empty in two more hours. Maybe it would be best if Lieutenant Tran just disappeared for a while. That would divert the cops and he could always kill him later after the plan was put into operation.

The colonel looked at Tran for a long moment. "Take him with us," he ordered.

In the right seat of Dragon One Zero, Jumal Mugabe bent over his sensor console and studied his instrument readouts. He reached out and flicked on the video camera in the ship's nose and dialed in the maximum magnification on the lens. While he was occupied with that, Wolff kept dodging the Griffin in and out of the concrete canyons of downtown Seattle. He was being careful not to expose them to a direct line of sight from the Space Needle for more than a few seconds at a time. "What do you see?" the pilot asked.

"Not much," Mugabe replied. "I'm on max magnification and all I can see are a couple of guys standing behind the windows. It looks like they're packing assault rifles, but I can't see what kind."

He checked the readouts briefly. "I'm getting too much background clutter on the doppler readout, so I can't tell how many people are in there."

He checked the defensive information readout on the tac

screen HUD. "The good news is that I don't have any lasers showing and no signs of radar, so they may not have spotted us yet."

"They've got us all right," Wolff said, banking his ship around the corner of the Ranier Bank Building. Fighting the erratic wind currents between the skyscrapers was making this a little more interesting than he had expected. One false move and they'd wind up sticking out of the side of a highrise condo or office building.

"Those jerks know the Griffins are in town," Wolff said. "And they'll have someone posted to keep an eye out for us."

"So, what do we do now?" Mugabe asked. "You want to try to get in a little closer and see if I can get a more accurate head count?"

Wolff shook his head. "No, we try that and we might get a Viper up our tail. I think we'd just better stay under cover while I call Buzz and see what he wants to do about this."

"Dragon Control," he radioed. "This is Dragon One Zero, let me talk to Command One."

"Command One, go."

"This is One Zero," Wolff replied. "They've really got us over a barrel on this one, Chief. There's no way that we can sneak up on that thing. Zoomie's got his work cut out for him."

"Command One, copy. Maintain your observation position till I get back to you."

"One Zero, copy."

CHAPTER 12

The Emerald Suite

Mai Lin put down the radio microphone and turned to the mayor. "For your sake, I hope your federal friends take us seriously," she said. "Otherwise, you're the first one who's going to be killed."

"For God's sake, why me!" the stunned politician asked in disbelief.

"Why you?" the dark haired Oriental beauty sneered. "Why you? Because I was ordered to do everything in my power to try to make a real man out of you and it sickened me, that's why. Also, your usefulness to us has ended. You are readily expendable." She waved a hand toward the stunned delegates, "But they are not."

One of the terrorists rattled off something in Vietnamese and pointed out the window of the revolving restaurant. In the distance, Johnson saw the dark, sleek shape of a Tac Force Griffin flitting in and out behind the tops of the city's skyscrapers.

Mai Lin and the apparent leader of the terrorists ran to the window and looked out. The man spun around, rattled off something in Vietnamese and a terrorist still dressed in his waiter's uniform ran out of the room.

"You may live through this after all," Mai said with a laugh as she turned to face the mayor. "It looks like the Tac Force is taking us seriously and are keeping their distance. For once, they aren't trying to play the hero."

Now Johnson had something else to worry about. He knew how the TPF operated. He had followed their exploits closely and he knew that they never negotiated in hostage situations. Even if it cost the lives of the hostages, they would not bargain and they never gave in to terrorists. He knew that the lone Griffin staying well out of the way was not the only chopper they had in Seattle. He had a sinking feeling in the pit of his stomach that the rest of them would arrive before too long with their guns blazing.

He looked around the room, trying to find a place to hide when they did appear.

Back at the Dragon Flight TOC, the Seattle police chief showed up with the plans for the Space Needle. "I also brought the city engineer," he said, giving Buzz a mini-hard disk. "And one of the restaurant managers if you need information on the exact layout inside."

"Good," Buzz said, slipping the disk into the computer. He quickly called up the plans on the screen. "Let's take a look at this thing."

As impressive as the Space Needle was from the ground, it was even more impressive when you were able to look inside and see how it was constructed. With Zumwald and Avila looking over his shoulder, Buzz scrolled through the engineering diagram. A slender tripod tower rose five hundred feet from the ground. In the center of the tower was a triangular elevator shaft carrying three cars.

"How many people can those elevators carry?" Zumwald asked.

"Twenty-five," the engineer answered. "And there are also stairs going up there too."

The tower terminated at the revolving, flying-saucer-like top 138 feet in diameter. Buzz called up the plan for the four level top itself next. The Emerald Suite took up half of the lower level, sharing the space with another restaurant and a huge kitchen. The next level was mainly structural, but contained offices and maintenance storage rooms. Next came the observation deck and gift shop level. The restaurant and observation levels were separated by a ring extending some twenty-two feet past the windows. This halo, as it was called, had sun louvers built into the top side that shaded the restaurants on the level below. Then under the sloping roof was the environmental and elevator machinery. The roof was topped with a fifty foot spire containing an aircraft warning beacon.

The Space Needle was an engineering marvel, but it was also a bitch of a place to try to sneak into.

"Okay," Buzz said, looking at the other officers. "How are we going to do this?"

"How about the elevators?" Chief Williams asked.

Zumwald shook his head and pointed to the elevator terminal on the plans. "Won't work. All it takes is one guy with an assault rifle guarding that and he can hold off an army."

"Also," the engineer broke in. "They can turn the elevators off from the top."

"The same thing goes for the stairs," Zumwald pointed out. "We try that and we're dead meat."

"Can't you just wait them out?" the restaurant manager asked hopefully. He was having visions of trying to clean up after a small war in his establishment.

Buzz snorted. "Wait them out? In a restaurant? It'd take 'em a year to starve to death up there, you ought to know that. They also said that they're going to start killing the hostages at three."

"How about a vertical envelopment?" Zumwald asked, a look of excitement coming over his face.

"Keep talking," Buzz frowned.

"Are there any windows in the roof of that thing?" the

Tac Platoon leader asked the engineer.

"No," the engineer answered. "The only windows are around the sides."

"Well," the Tac Platoon leader continued. "The way I see it, that's the only way we can sneak up on them, from above. If we come straight down on top of 'em, they won't be able to see us coming. Particularly with that halo blocking the view upward from the restaurant."

"You might have something there," Buzz said thoughtfully. "What exactly do you have in mind?"

Zumwald studied the plans for a moment. "Well, I was thinking that me and a few of the guys could go up with one of the choppers and have them let us out on the top." He tapped the screen.

"Then what?"

Zumwald grinned. "Then we'll just do the usual 'in through the windows' number and ace 'em before they know what's happening."

"Don't forget that those windows are five hundred feet above the ground," Buzz reminded him.

"I know," he smiled slowly. "That's what's going to make this one much more fun than usual."

Buzz shook his head. Zoomie was off on one of his adrenaline trips again. It was one of the craziest ideas he had ever heard. But it was also the only thing he had heard today that made any sense.

"Okay, let's do it," he agreed. "Just how do you want to work it?"

Zumwald studied the plan for a few minutes and then began to outline his assault plan. When he was finished, Buzz had a couple of questions about the details, but he approved the plan.

"One last thing," Zumwald said. "Since we don't know where the hostages are being held, I'd like permission to use Glaser safety slugs in our MP-5s."

Buzz thought for a moment. The Glaser safety slug

ammunition had been designed specifically for police work in situations like this when there was a danger of a bullet punching through a man and hitting someone else or ricocheting from a hard surface. The Glaser bullets were like small shotgun shells, but the individual pellets inside the projectile did not come out until the round hit a body. Then the bullet opened up and the pellets tore a gaping hole in the target. A 9mm Glaser would hit a target with the power of a .44 Magnum hollow point round, but would not exit out the back of the victim and hit someone else. Also, it would not ricochet.

"If the terrorists were smart," Zumwald explained his request. "They'll have the hostages close to them to use as cover. Using the Glaser ammunition might hold down the number of friendly casualties if we get into a real tight contest up there, sir."

"But if you do hit a friendly by mistake," Buzz pointed out. "The Glasers will damn near make sure that he or she dies."

Zumwald shrugged. "This isn't a tea party we're going to, Captain. There's always the chance that some of those people will get hit no matter what kind of ammunition we use. I'm more concerned about putting the terrorists down before they can shoot anyone, my people or the hostages."

"Okay," Buzz finally said. "Do it, but for Christ's sakes, be careful."

"We'll try, sir."

Zumwald quickly printed out a hard copy of the plans of the restaurant level of the Space Needle and headed out the door at a dead run. It was going to take a little while to put this thing together and they were running out of time before the deadline arrived.

An hour later, Wolff flared out and put his Griffin

down right at the edge of the tarmac where Zoomie was waiting with nine men from the Tac Platoon. Bent over to clear the spinning rotor blades, the men ran up to the side of the ship, slid open the side doors and scrambled into the passenger compartment in the rear of the chopper.

Normally, the Griffin only carried six fully equipped officers. But if this operation was going to have any chance of success at all, they needed at least ten men. Wolff would just have to make it work.

Zumwald and five of the assault team took their places inside on the canvas jump seats and the other four cops sat in the open doors with their feet hanging down over the side of the ship.

The Tac Platoon leader took the spare flight helmet from his seat, slipped it on his head and plugged the cord into the intercom jack. He could have called Wolff on his own built-in helmet radio. But since there was a good chance that the terrorists had a police frequency monitor, this whole operation would be done without using their radios until they made contact with the terrorists.

"We're go, Wolfman," he called up to the pilot.

"Copy," the pilot called back. "Tell 'em to hang on back there, Zoomie."

The ship was overloaded by almost a thousand pounds so Wolff hit the over-rev switch on the turbine governor as he pulled pitch to the rotor blades and nudged forward on the cyclic. The Griffin rose sluggishly into the air in a ground effect hover. Wolff kept the tail high as he taxied out onto the runway and started off in a classic gunship takeoff. As soon as his airspeed came up, he slowly fed in more pitch and the chopper rose up into the air.

He kicked down on the rudder pedal, going into a gentle banking turn as he headed out over Puget Sound away from the Space Needle. The ship climbed slowly to five thousand feet and he switched over to Scramcom tactical communications channel and keyed his throat mike.

"Dragon Control," he radioed. "This is One Zero, I am Code One at five thousand."

"Control, copy. Stand by."

"One Zero, copy."

In the rear compartment of the Griffin, Zumwald's men checked over their equipment one last time. This was the trickiest operation they had done to date and, one little item that was not working at a hundred percent could get someone killed long before they even got into range of the terrorists' guns.

The Tac cops were dressed in their black SWAT uniforms with black armored jackets and assault harnesses. Since they wouldn't have to do any running around on the ground, Zumwald had ordered them to wear the full set of Kevlar and ceramic armor inserts in both their jackets and their uniforms themselves. Wearing the full armor inserts dramatically restricted their mobility, but this time, they needed the extra protection.

Black Kevlar helmets with full Lexan face shields and nose filters completed their uniforms. The helmets contained voice activated commo gear and earphone plugs allowing the ten men to talk to one another even over the roar of gunfire. The helmet radios could also be used switched over to talk to the choppers and the Tactical Operations Center.

All ten men carried 9mm H and K MP-5 submachineguns. The MP-5s could put out 800 rounds a minute, emptying a 30 round magazine in under two and a half seconds. Backing up the MP-5s they all carried Glock 10mm pistols. If they had to use the pistols, they wanted first round kills and the powerful 10mm round would stop a grizzly bear in his tracks and knock him over on his back. Also, since their MP-5s were loaded with Glasers and could not penetrate walls or doors, the hard nosed pistol slugs would let them take out any terrorists who took cover behind any hard surface.

Zumwald had a big grin on his face as he snapped his shoulder strap down over the sling to his MP-5 sub-machinegun and took a final hitch on the right leg strap of his Swiss Chair rapelling harness. He could feel the adrenaline start pumping throughout his body.

Missions like this were why Zoomie had joined the Tac Force. Mountain climbing, skydiving and static jumping hadn't been enough for him. He had wanted bigger and better adrenaline highs and that was exactly what the Tac Force gave him. Every time he went up against a situation like this, he'd stay high for days.

Assuming he lived.

Mayor Johnson looked up when one of the Red Fist Commandos shouted and pointed out the window. Flying right at the top of the Space Needle came three speeding Tac Force Griffins. At the last possible moment, the shark-like ships banked away and went into an orbit five hundred meters away from the restaurant. He could see the Griffins' gun turrets pointed right at them and the helmeted heads of the gunners looking out of their door windows.

He leaped to his feet and ran to the window, waving his arms trying to signal them to go away. One of the terrorists slammed him down on the floor and shoved the muzzle of his assault rifle in his face. Mai saw what was happening and said something to the man in Vietnamese. The terrorist pulled back his weapon.

"You do that again," the woman said. "And I may not be able to stop them from killing you."

"But I was just trying to wave them away," he wailed, his eyes following the weapon.

"Just sit down and shut up if you want to live," Mai

97

snapped.

Johnson swallowed hard and sat back down. His mind was racing. In just a few minutes, all hell was going to break loose in here and he needed a place to hide.

CHAPTER 13

TPF Tactical Operations Center

Buzz was watching the display on his tac screen when one of the communication specialists at the other end of the room called over to him.

"We've got us a real problem here, sir," the man said, pointing to one of the five TV monitors tuned into the local television stations. The small screen showed a low angle, long range shot of the Griffin choppers circling the top of the Space Needle.

"When One Zero drops down over the top of the Needle, they're going to pick him up with their cameras and, if the terrorists have a TV set turned on, they going to see him coming for sure."

Buzz keyed his throat mike and radioed Lieutenant Avila, the officer in charge of the units blockading the streets around the Seattle Center. "Command Three, this is Command One, shut that damned TV camera down."

"This is Command Three, which one?" Avila asked. "There are four mobile TV units here."

"The Turner Network," the communications specialist answered the question.

Buzz gritted his teeth, it would be TNT again. They were always the first to arrive on the scene trying to get their cameras right under the gun muzzles anytime something like this was going on. They were damned good at what they did, but right now they were getting in the way again.

99

"Turner Network," he transmitted curtly. "Shut them down now."

"Command Three, copy."

Avila looked behind him and saw the TNT mobile van parked down at the end of the block. The reporter was up at the barricade doing a voice over while the long range cameras tracked the Griffins circling the Space Needle. He knew that if he went over there and asked the guy to turn it off, all he would get from him was a ration of crap about the press and First Amendment rights. Under the Tactical Police Act, they had to shut their cameras down if the TPF requested that they do it. But the reporters always argued about it anyway and often demanded that the cops produce a court order before they'd comply.

Avila didn't have time to screw around with any of that right now; Wolff was due to drop out of the sky any second. He turned to the Tac Force sharpshooter standing by the barricade. "Take out that microwave dish antenna," he ordered, pointing to the TNT van.

The shooter smiled. "No sweat."

The sniper snuggled his cheek into the stock of his Styer 7.62mm sniper's rifle, sighted in on the center of the white transmission dish and focused his ranging scope on the wave guide. The silenced rifle spat once and a puff of dust sprang from the center of the dish.

"There," the marksman said with a smile as he lowered his rifle. "That ought to do it, Lieutenant."

"Command One," Avila called back to the TOC. "This is Three, they should be off the air now."

"Command One, copy, they are. Good work."

"This is Three, what about the other networks?"

"They're okay," Buzz radioed back. "TNT was the only one in position to pick them up."

"Three copy."

Avila looked back up in the sky above the Space

Needle. A thousand feet above the saucer top, Wolff's Dragon One Zero hung motionless in the sky. He could barely make out the six dark shapes hanging a hundred feet under her skids and he held his breath. As he watched, the chopper slowly started descending straight down over the sharp spire of the Space Needle.

The Air-Ground officer keyed his mike and transmitted to the other three choppers doing the Indians-circling-the-wagons routine around the restaurant. "Dragons Two, Three and Four, this is Command Three. Keep 'em occupied! One Zero's coming down now!"

The three Griffins suddenly stopped circling and went into a hover, their noses pointing in toward the Space Needle. Their chin turrets swept from side to side as if they were looking for a target to open up on. That maneuver was guaranteed to get someone's attention in there.

In the right seat of Dragon One Four, Sandra Revell switched the ammo feed for her 40mm grenade launcher over to a mix of flash-bang grenades and stun gas, three flash-bang rounds for one gas. She dialed in the ball ammunition for the Chain gun as well. With hostages in there, she couldn't use the big gun unless something went desperately wrong, but she wanted to have it ready anyway.

She carefully studied the sensor readouts on her attack screen so she wouldn't be tempted to make the mistake of looking up to watch Wolff's descent. All it would take would be for one of the terrorists to see that the pilots were watching the sky over the Space Needle and the critical element of surprise would be lost.

Jack Zumwald was one of the six men hanging on

the rapelling ropes a hundred feet under the hovering Griffin. He would have liked to have dropped all ten men of his assault team at the same time. It would be faster and give him more firepower in case they had a nasty reception, but the chopper could only accommodate six ropes at once so it had to be done in two drops.

The down blast of the rotors buffeted his head as the chopper slowly descended over the top of the Space Needle. He had made hundreds of rapells from hovering choppers before, but this was a first for him. He and his men weren't rapelling this time, they were hanging on the ends of the ropes while the chopper slowly lowered them down onto the top of the Space Needle.

This part of it was easy, the trick was to guide Wolff's descent so they would hit their target, the spire on the top of the Needle.

Since he was still maintaining radio silence, he could only use hand signals to guide the pilot. It was risky to do it that way, but he had no choice. "Little more," he said to himself as he signaled Wolff by pumping his arm up and down. "More, more . . . Hold it!"

He spread both arms to signal the stop and then reached out for the spire. A sudden gust of wind caught the hovering chopper, slamming him into it. He grunted in pain, but managed to get a firm grip and hold on. He quickly tied the end of the rope to the spire and then started climbing down to the ledge at the base. The five men with him gained handholds too and soon joined him.

Zumwald paused for a moment listening to see if he could hear anything indicating that anyone inside had heard them land. As he had expected, everything was quiet and he gave the hand signal for the rest of the assault team to make their descent.

The last four men quickly rapelled down the ropes and caught onto the spire. They released the ropes and, in seconds, they too were down at the base. The ten men spaced themselves evenly around the north side of the spire, took the short nylon ropes they carried from their assault harnesses and tied them to the base of the spire. Each man found a precisely measured, pre-tied loop close to the ends of the ropes and hooked it into the carbineers on the front of their Swiss Chair rapelling harness.

There was a sheer vertical drop from the base of the spire to the sloping roof itself and the raiders slowly lowered themselves down, being careful to make as little noise as possible. Once down, they turned to face out toward the edge of the roof and gave their leader a "Go" signal.

When each man was ready, Zoomie keyed his helmet radio for the first time. "This is Command Two," he transmitted. "One, two, three, go!"

The Griffins hovering outside the restaurant immediately opened up with their grenade launchers, sweeping their turrets from side to side. The 40mm flash-bang grenades smashed through the windows and exploded inside the restaurant with a blinding flash and an ear splitting thunderclap. According to the ordnance manuals, the bright flashes and loud detonations would blind and deafen everyone in the room.

The instant the choppers fired, Zoomie took a two handed grip on his MP-5 and screamed "Airborne!"

The ten Tac Cops launched themselves down the sloping top of the Space Needle, running as hard as they could for the edge of the slippery concrete roof. When they reached the edge, they didn't even try to stop themselves. In fact, they leaped as far out into space as they could, trailing the ropes behind them like parachute static lines. For this to work, they had to jump past the edge of the halo that extended twenty-two feet from the edge of the roof.

From the ground, it looked like all ten of them were committing mass suicide.

As their falling bodies passed the edge of the sharp halo, the ropes pulled tight against the base of the spire and jerked the falling cops to a sudden stop in mid-air. Then gravity took over.

When they fell, the ropes caught on the edge of the rim of the saucer and snapped them into a downward swing.

If the ropes had been measured properly and were exactly the right length, the swing would send Zumwald and the assault team feet first, right through the side windows of the Emerald Suite. If the ropes were either too long or too short, however, they would smash into the ledges above or below the windows. Zumwald had taken the measurements from the engineering plans himself and he was confident that this would work. If he had screwed up, though, he probably wouldn't live long enough to realize it.

As Zumwald flew through the air, he tensed himself for his impact with the window. He knew that his Lexan face shield and full body armor would protect him from the thick plate glass, but he still closed his eyes at the last moment. His boots crashed through with a shower of jagged glass and he fell into the smoke-filled restaurant.

"Police!" he shouted. "Get down!"

Zumwald was only vaguely aware of the other cops crashing through the windows on either side of him as he hit the rope release of his harness and snapped his MP-5 up into a firing position. A round sang past his head and he went into an adrenaline-fueled overdrive.

Falling into a crouch, he triggered off a short burst from the MP-5 and saw the Glaser slugs slam a body back against one of the interior walls.

One down!

Many of the terrorists had been stunned by the flash bang grenades, but a few of them still wanted to fight. The high pitched chatter of the terrorists' M-25s was answered by the bark of the MP-5s and the boom of the 10mm Glocks. The black-clad figures of the assault team were a blur as they raced through the restaurant in a ballet of death, flame spitting from the muzzles of their MPs.

Spinning around to the other side, Zumwald drew down on another moving figure he had caught in his peripheral vision. But the instant before he fired, he saw the man's head turn bright red when he took a Glaser round in the face from another one of the assault team.

Two down!

Rolling off to the side, the lieutenant saw a man break for cover behind a serving cart and triggered off a long burst at him. Most of the Glaser rounds impacted harmlessly against the metal cart, but one of them hit the man in the chest, pulping his lungs and heart.

Three down!

As he dropped behind a chair to change magazines in his MP, Zumwald caught a glimpse of a terrorist drawing down on him. He threw himself off to the side as the muzzle of the terrorist's assault rifle flashed flame. The burst of 5.56mm slugs slammed into his body armor, throwing him back against a table. One round ricocheted off his face shield, snapping his head back.

Stunned by the impact, Zumwald tried to raise himself. When the terrorist moved to fire again, his combat instincts took over. Swinging his MP-5 up with one hand, he triggered off the last four rounds remaining in the magazine, dropped the empty weapon and scrambled for the Glock pistol in the holster on his hip.

Three of the MP's slugs hit harmlessly against the wall. Only one of the 9mm Glasers found the target. The round hit the terrorist's upper arm, smashing the bone and shredding the muscle. But this time, it was not enough to take the fight out of him. With a scream of rage, the Vietnamese tried to shift his rifle to the other hand.

But before he could fire again, Zumwald triggered off three quick shots. The powerful 10mm hollow point slugs slammed the terrorist off his feet and put him down for good.

Zumwald fought to catch his breath as he dropped the empty magazine from his MP and slammed a fresh one into the magazine well. Slamming the bolt forward to chamber a round, he looked to see how badly he had been hit. The cloth cover of his body armor was torn where the terrorist's bullets had ripped through it, but the plates seemed to be intact. Taking a deep breath, he poked his head around the edge of the chair looking for his next target, but the battle was over.

The only men still on their feet were wearing the black uniforms of the Tac Force assault team. Even through the Red First Commandos had been armed with the Army's latest hi-tech weapons, they had proven to be no match for Zumwald and his trained men.

As quickly as it had began, it was all over. The sudden silence was deafening.

A second later, the stillness was broken by a scream of pain. "Stay down!" Zoomie shouted, looking around for his men.

"Report!" he ordered. "One, clear!" came an answering call in his headphones as his team members reported their status to the platoon commander. "Two, clear! Three, clear! Four, clear! . . ."

Zumwald slowly got to his feet, his heart still pounding and his finger hovering over the trigger. It was over and he was alive.

He switched his radio over to the Tac Force command frequency. "Command One," he transmitted. "This is Command Two, we're clear up here. Get the medics going ASAP."

"This is Command One, copy," Buzz called back. "What are the casualties?"

"We're still counting, wait one."

CHAPTER 14

The Space Needle

While Buzz waited by the radio, Zumwald started counting the dead and wounded. The inside of the Emerald Suite looked like a slaughterhouse, bright red pools of fresh blood were everywhere. Bodies in camouflage uniforms and dark business suits lay scattered throughout the banquet room. His men were helping the survivors to their feet and moving the wounded to the elevator terminal where the medics had arrived to treat them.

The assault team officer took a notepad from his pants pocket and started tallying the butcher's bill.

Buzz wanted his damage report ASAP, but Zumwald checked on the damage to his team first. Considering what they had been through, he was surprised to see that so few of them had been hurt. One of his men had been cut by a jagged piece of glass that had slipped past the side of his ceramic thigh plate and cut deep into his leg. Another man had been hit with a round that had penetrated the shoulder plate of his armored jacket. Those were the only casualties in his team and now he had to check on the hostages. He was afraid that they had not fared as well as his men had.

Again, though, he was pleasantly surprised. Only two of the delegates were dead. He would make sure that their wounds were examined to see who was responsible for their deaths, but they both looked like they had been killed by the terrorists, not his own men. Another seven of them had been wounded, but only one of them seriously. They had gotten off lightly.

The terrorists, however, had been cut to pieces. Most of them were dead, the Glaser slugs had made sure of that, but a few had survived who could be patched up and interrogated later. He had his men separate the wounded terrorists from the ex-hostages and put them under guard.

Next, he checked on the restaurant's staff. Most of them had been locked away in the kitchen when the takeover had occurred so they had taken no gunshot wounds. A few of them had been roughed up, however, and required first aid.

That left only one body he could not account for, a beautiful, young Oriental woman with long black hair. She had a shocked expression on her face and a thin trickle of blood running from the corner of her mouth. She wasn't wearing a name tag, and Zumwald hoped to God that she hadn't been one of the delegates.

A man in a business suit staggered up to the woman's body. "Bitch," he spat. "This was all her fault."

"Who was she?" Zumwald asked. "And who are you?"

"I'm Ralph Johnson," he said. "The mayor of Seattle. She was one of my aides, but she was working for them. She planned this whole thing."

"What do you mean?"

"She talked me into having this lunch up here," the mayor answered. "She offered to arrange everything and now I know why." His voice grew shriller. "When they took over, she was one of their leaders. She even . . ."

Zumwald took the mayor's arm. "Mister Mayor," he

109

said cutting the man off in mid-sentence. "I think you'd better check in with the medics." The last thing in the world he needed right now was to have to deal with a hysterical local politician.

"But," Johnson sputtered. "You don't understand, she . . ."

Zumwald led the mayor over to one of the medics. "This is Mayor Johnson," he said. "Can you check him over?"

"Sure thing."

Now that he had the body count, Zumwald called the information into the TOC. While he was on the radio, the medics cleared the casualties, both terrorist and delegate alike, and the cops quickly escorted the survivors down the elevators.

When Buzz had the data, Zumwald walked through the Emerald Suite and continued to survey the wreckage, both material and human. Far too many of the hostages had been hurt, but he was proud of his men for having saved as many of them as they had. It had been the most difficult hostage save they had ever pulled off.

He walked over to where two of his men guarded the three wounded terrorists. "How are these maggots doing?" he asked.

"They'll live, Lieutenant."

"Good," Zumwald replied. "I'm looking forward to having a little chat with them later."

"Yes, sir," the cop grinned.

Now that it was finally over, Zumwald could stop for a moment. He fingered the tears in his armored vest. That had been close, too damned close. He suppressed a shudder and looked out the broken window at the rapelling ropes dangling off the roof. Now that it was over, he could hardly believe that he had actually done that.

"Hey," he radioed to his men. "Let's get this whole thing wrapped up here. I need a beer."

"You buying?" someone asked.

"No way."

Buzz sat at the tac screen in the TOC as the reports continued to pour in from the Space Needle. Two of the hostages had been killed and another seven wounded. Nine of the terrorists were dead, the remaining three wounded and captured. One female mayor's aide was dead. One fancy restaurant had been thoroughly trashed. One TV transmission dish was seriously wounded. All told, it had been a messy, but very successful operation, considering the circumstances.

Buzz was not wasting any time, however, congratulating himself for a job well done. Something about this whole thing just didn't make any sense to him. For one thing, it was insanity for the terrorists to have taken the hostages while they were in the top of the Space Needle. On the surface the idea was sound, it had made it damnably difficult for the Tac Force to even attempt a rescue. And had it not been for Zoomie's crazy idea, a stand off with the terrorists might have gone on for days.

At the same time, holding the hostages up there had also made it impossible for the terrorists to escape if something went wrong. In his experience, people who took hostages always planned a way out, but as far as he could see, this had been a suicide mission.

But for what? What had the terrorists gained by holding the hostages for three short hours? Other than gaining the undivided attention of every single cop in the Greater Seattle area.

The main question was still just who in the hell

111

were these guys? Not even Washington had information about a Red Fist Commando terrorist group. They had to be local boys and this whole thing was some kind of operation designed to tie up the police while something else was going on.

The question was what? The obvious answer was giving the Boa Hoa time to move the stolen warhead. The second question was, had the hostage incident lasted long enough for Dong to have done whatever it was he had planned to do with the missile.

Buzz glanced over to the chronometer readout on the top of the screen, 1523 hours, he still had time to wrap this thing up and run the sweep in "Little Saigon" tonight as he had planned. Maybe the Space Needle incident hadn't lasted long enough for Dong to have moved the missile yet. Maybe he could still recapture it.

He keyed his throat mike, "Command Two, Command Three, Dragon One Zero, this is Command One. Report back to the TOC ASAP."

When Zumwald, Avila and Wolff called back to say that they were on the way, Buzz turned to Ruby. "Tell the Seattle PD that I want 'Little Saigon' cordoned off ASAP, no one goes in or out without being searched. Particularly vehicles."

"Yes, sir."

"Also," Buzz continued. "See if the field office has found their lieutenant yet," he asked. "I need to talk to this young man."

"Yes, sir."

Buzz got up and walked over to the big map of Seattle on the wall and studied the "Little Saigon" area. He wondered what little surprises Dong was going to pull on them tonight. It made his work easier if he could just look at the situation and not get involved with the personalities. But this time, he was willing to make an exception.

This Dong was dangerous and he was one guy that Buzz really wanted to see put out of business as soon as possible.

Lieutenant Tran had absolutely no idea where he was being taken. He had not been able to see anything with the blindfold and he had no idea how much time had passed since he had been led from Dong's headquarters and put in the back of a truck. It had been only a short ride until he was taken from the truck and thrown into the hold of a hovercraft. He had tried to count the seconds, so he could keep track of the time and have some idea where he was being taken, but that had proved to be impossible.

His office would have started looking for him by now, but they wouldn't have a chance in hell of finding him. Not for the first time, he wished that he had been a little more cautious this morning. There was a lot to be said for being a hard-charging young cop who had a reputation for getting things done. But there was more to be said for taking his head out of the sand before he ran off on something like this without having a backup available. He had violated the number one rule of undercover police work by trying to go it alone, and he was afraid that he was going to pay for it with his life.

The roar of the hovercraft's impeller fans took on a different note and the craft seemed to be slowing down. Wherever it was that Dong was taking him, it looked like they had finally arrived. While he hadn't been able to keep an accurate time count, he felt that they had been on the water for at least an hour. But since he was in the Puget Sound, that wasn't much help. He could be anywhere from Canada to any one of a hundred islands, large and small, that dotted the northern Washington coastline.

He felt the skirts of the hovercraft brush against the wave tops as the vessel slowed even further. The side of the hull scraped against something and the props went into reverse to stop dead. The impellers stopped too and the hull sank into the water. He heard feet on the deck above scamper to tie the craft up to a dock.

A few minutes later, two Boa Hoa came down and escorted him up onto the deck.

"Take his blindfold off," he heard Dong say.

Tran blinked his eyes in the sudden sunlight and saw that they were tied up to a dock on what looked to be an island. That was not surprising, an island was a perfect hideout. The question was, which island?

"You are probably wondering where you are," the gang leader said.

"As a matter of fact, I am."

Dong smiled slowly. "I will tell you," he said. "Because you will never leave here alive, it does not matter if you know. You are on Gray's Island."

"The prison island?" Tran looked inland. Behind the thin covering of trees along the shoreline was a large, squat, gray concrete building, the abandoned Harrington federal prison. Tran didn't know much about the prison other than it had been abandoned very soon after it had been built because of some environmental law-suit.

It seemed that there was some rare species of spotted sea gull that used the island as a nesting site. And since the gull was on the endangered species list, the federal courts ruled that the island had to be abandoned. It didn't matter that millions of taxpayers' dollars had been spent building it, it had had to be abandoned, buildings and all. Very little had been salvaged. The environmentalists had argued that tearing down the prison would have been more destructive to the birds than to leave it standing.

However, now it looked like the sea gulls had new neighbors and Tran didn't think that Dong and his gang were all that concerned about a few dumbass birds. He almost laughed when he thought what the environmentalists would do if they knew that a nuclear egg was nesting here with their precious sea gulls.

"Now what happens to me?" Tran asked his captor.

"You come with me as my guest," Dong answered. "You will be allowed to live a little longer."

"Gee thanks." Tran tried to sound sarcastic.

"You may not thank me when you see your accommodations," Dong replied. "But remember that your people built this place."

Tran's heart sank. Harrington Prison had been built as a no frills, maximum security facility for the most dangerous prisoners in America. It was considered impossible to escape from and, if Dong had somehow gotten access to the cells' electronic key codes, he would be there for good.

It was a short walk to the main gate of the fenced compound. Once inside the building, Dong ordered his men to lock Tran in one of the basement cells.

"One question first," the cop said.

"And, what is that?"

"What are you going to do with that warhead?"

"You will find out if you live long enough. Take him away," Dong told the guards in Vietnamese.

Tran was led below and put into the first cell along the corridor. As he had feared, it was a two-man maximum security cell with an electronic lock on the barred door. Even if the power was cut to the compound, there was no way that he was going to get out

115

of there. Since he was in the basement, there was no window for him to see out and also no way that he could signal to anyone who might be outside.

Once the guards resumed their positions, the only sound Tran could hear was the sea gulls.

CHAPTER 15

The Coast Guard Base

Back at the Coast Guard base, Zero Hour for the sweep had arrived, eighteen hundred hours. The crews of the four Griffin choppers were strapped into the cockpits of their machines waiting for the word from the C and C for the evening's operation, Wolff and Mugabe in Dragon One Zero.

In his ship, Wolff impatiently watched the chronometer in the instrument panel. When the digital readout clicked over to eighteen hundred hours, he triggered the switch to his throat mike. "Dragon Flight," he radioed. "This is One Zero, crank 'em."

As the rogers came in from the three other pilots, Mugabe began the turbine startup checklist. As Wolff's gloved fingers flew over the Griffin's switches and controls, he called out each item to his co-pilot.

"Battery, on. Internal power, on. Inverter switch, off. RPM warning light, on. Fuel, both main and start, on. RPM governor, decrease."

Mugabe looked over his shoulder to check both sides of the ship. "Rotor, clear. Light it!"

Reaching down with his right hand, Wolff twisted the throttle open to Flight Idle and pulled the starting trigger on the collective control stick. In the rear of the bird, the portside GE turbine burst into life with a screeching whine and the smell of burned kerosene. Over their heads, the forty foot main rotor slowly began to pick up speed. As soon as the portside turbine was

117

running at 40 percent RPM he switched over and fired up the other one.

As the turbine RPMs built up and the rotor blades came up to speed, the pilot held the throttle at flight idle and watched the exhaust gas temperature and RPM gauges. Everything was in the green.

He twisted the throttle all the way up against the stop. The whine built to a bone-shaking scream as the turbines ran up all the way to 6,000 RPM. Everything was still in the green.

He flipped the RPM governor switch to increase and the turbines screamed even higher at 6700 RPMs. Everything was still green.

Wolff backed off on the throttle, and waited as the other three Griffins called in their status to him.

"One Four, ready."

"One Two, we're go."

"One Three, turning."

Switching radio channels, Wolff keyed his mike, "Dragon Control, this is Dragon One Zero, Dragon Flight is ready for take off."

"This is Control, you are cleared for take off. Orbit at five thousand and contact Air Ground Control on tac channel two."

"One Zero, copy," Wolff transmitted.

He switched back to the chopper-to-chopper channel and twisted his throttle up against the stop. The twin GE turbines screamed under full power, shaking the Griffin's airframe as the four-bladed rotor accelerated to full RPM. With all the Coast Guardsmen and head-quarters types watching them, Wolff wanted to make this look good. Real good.

"Dragon Flight," he called to the other machines. "This is One Zero. On my command," he paused. "Pull pitch, now!"

As if tied together with a string, the four sleek, dark

118

blue Griffins lifted their tails and rose into the air as one. With Wolff's One Zero in the lead, they cleared the end of the runway, turned east and flew into the sunset like seahawks returning to their roosts in the islands.

Dragon Flight was on the wing.

As the Griffins climbed up into the sky, the police units on the ground made a final check of their equipment and moved into their launch positions. If the Boa Hoa wanted a fight tonight, they were going to get it. But this time, however, it was not going to be a one-sided battle like it had been the night before. The men of the Seattle PD SWAT teams were anxious to avenge the deaths of their brother officers and they were armed to the teeth.

As police officers, they did not want to see another bloody firefight in the streets of the city they had sworn to protect. But if that was the way the Boa Hoa wanted it, they were not going to be caught off guard again. One way or the other, "Little Saigon" was going to be brought back under the rule of law and order.

Lieutenant Zumwald's Tac Platoon was also suited up for the sweep. The earlier Space Needle hostage operation had just been an appetizer for Zoomie and his men. They were ready to do some serious law enforcement.

They had suited up in urban combat camouflage uniforms, a dazzle pattern of black, gray, and off-white jagged stripes. Over that, they wore their Kevlar body armor jackets with ceramic inserts covering their vital areas. The flak jackets were covered with the same camouflage material as their uniforms and had pouches to hold their spare magazines and tactical equipment. Their Kevlar helmets were fitted with built-in commo equipment and bulletproof Lexan face shields and nose filters.

The Tac Platoons were broken down into five man tactical teams for tonight's mission. And, since they were going up against a street fighting scenario, three of the men were armed with H and K MP-5 9mm submachineguns, one man carried a Styer SSG 7.62mm sniper's rifle and the fifth, a 12 gauge Franchi automatic shotgun/grenade launcher. No matter what tactical situation they encountered tonight, that weapons mix would let them take care of it.

Since two of his people were out from the wounds they had taken in the Space Needle rescue, Zumwald assumed command of one of the tac teams himself.

"Okay, boys," he called out to his team. "Our ride is here. Lock and load!"

Not only were the Seattle PD SWAT teams and the TPF Tac Platoon on hand, but all four of the V-500 heavy patrol cars from the TPF Seattle field office had been rolled out to support the operation.

Although they were called a heavy patrol car, the V-500 was more armored riot vehicle than it was police patrol car. Descended from the Cadillac Gauge Commando armored car series, the amphibious, six wheel, armored vehicle was capable of carrying ten police officers plus a driver, a commander/gunner and a systems operator.

The heavies were armored to withstand fifty caliber armor-piercing ammunition and were fitted with a turret that mounted searchlights, a Chain gun and a grenade launcher. When the heavy firepower wasn't needed, the turret could be replaced with a water cannon for dispersing unarmed crowds and busting up demonstrations. Tonight, however, the high powered squirt guns had been replaced with the 25mm Chain gun turrets.

The heavies were also outfitted with the same commo gear and computer systems as the Griffins so they could be tac linked with the choppers as well as with the TPF

Tactical Operations Center. When the heavies rolled with the Griffins providing aircover, they were tied together into one single combat machine that could hold its own against many nation's military forces.

Climbing to five thousand feet over The Puget Sound, Wolff and Mugabe again saw the city below as a glittering panorama of tall buildings and bright colored lights. The ferries and hovercraft tied up at the piers in the harbor looked like models. He was able to clearly see the crowded streets and small shops of "Little Saigon." There was nothing to indicate that in just a few minutes, those streets would be ablaze with gunfire.

The other Griffins were orbiting well off to the side waiting to be sent in where they were needed, but because he was the Command and Control ship for the operation, Wolff flew close enough to see the police units moving in to surround "Little Saigon." Any minute now, Buzz would give them the word to move out and he would send the Griffins swarming over the target area,

On the ground, Buzz Corcran, Ruby Jenkins, and Ramon Avila were in the mobile tactical command vehicle, a heavy that had been converted to hold communications and computer equipment. Parked down a side street right at the edge of the operation area, Buzz watched the tactical map display screen as the units, both the Seattle PD and the Tac Force, moved into position. The map color coded each of the units and displayed their status and call signs giving him an instant picture of what was going on. When the tac units dismounted, their individual commo beacons would show him the location of each man as well. No commander had ever had as good a picture of his battlefield as Buzz Corcran did.

Once all the units were in place, Buzz spun around

in his chair and gave Ruby the word.

"Show time, Mom," he said. "Tell 'em to go to work."

"All units," she transmitted. "This is Dragon Control, commence operations."

At the call, Wolff keyed his throat mike. "Dragon One Four, this is One Zero, read 'em the riot act, Gunner."

"One Four, copy," Gunner Jennings answered as he dropped down out of the sky and aimed his ship for "Little Saigon." Keying his intercom, he turned to his systems operator. "Go full defensive, Legs."

Sandra Revell's gloved fingers flew over the counter-measures panel switching the chopper's mirror skin to full reflection and turned on the radar jamming module for extra protection. She knew that their opponents had Viper missiles, but they might have other nasty surprises as well. It never hurt to be cautious.

As Jennings dropped down over the tops of the buildings, Revell kept the fingers of her left hand poised over the decoy flare button while the right was on the turret weapons controls.

Lining up with the street that bordered the search area, Jennings flicked a switch and a recorded message began to play over the loud speaker system in the belly of the chopper.

"This is the United States Tactical Police," the loud-speakers blared. "This area has been declared a Federal Emergency Crime Area. All people are to open their doors to police and cooperate to the fullest. Anyone not obeying the police can be detained for questioning."

The message was played in Vietnamese and several other Asian languages as the chopper flew back and forth over the target area.

While One Four flew low over the rooftops below, Mugabe also went to full defensive, his sensors were seeking any sign of active anti-aircraft weapons, particularly the laser designators of Viper missiles. "So far, so good," he told Wolff.

"Let's hope it stays that way," the pilot replied grimly, watching Jennings's Griffin bank around for another run over "Little Saigon."

As soon as Dragon One Four had played the message several times, Mom relayed the order for the heavies to move out. "Heavy patrol units One through Four, move out now."

The drivers gunned their engines and the four heavies moved in from four different directions. They drove at a crawl, their turret weapons locked and loaded searching windows and rooftops for signs of anyone who wanted to play. Right behind the heavies, the Seattle police force moved in to search the shops and apartments along the crowded streets.

Initially, the mission went well, almost too well. The citizens opened their doors to the search units and nothing much out of the ordinary was found. A few drug stashes were confiscated and the owners given citations. One cache of stolen property was found and a big crack operation was put out of business.

It was just your typical garden variety, low level criminal activity that could be found in any large American city. So far, there was no sign of the powerful gang that controlled the area.

What the police didn't know was that Dong had been warned about the sweep and was more than ready for it.

Almost as soon as the operation had been decided upon, his agents in the mayor's office and Seattle police department had passed the word on to the gang leader. Dong had immediately evacuated most of his people to temporary hideouts outside "Little Saigon." While the Tac Force had been tied up with the hostage situation in the Space Needle, the Trident warhead was already on its way to his new island headquarters.

All that was left of the Boa Hoa in "Little Saigon" were some two dozen of Dong's best fighters. They were armed to the teeth with the stolen Army weapons and had vowed to fight to the death to tie up the police and give their leader time to make good his escape.

CHAPTER 16

"Little Saigon"

The first sign that the Boa Hoa had not completely abandoned "Little Saigon" was when a Scorpion anti-tank rocket streaked down from a roof top. It exploded with a blinding flash directly in front of one of the heavies.

Had the gunner taken the time to aim a little more carefully, he might have bagged the armored vehicle. Not even a V-500 could withstand a direct hit from the warhead of a Scorpion anti-tank missile. But the Boa Hoa gangster had gotten a little overanxious and he had missed. Now it was the heavy's turn.

The turret motor whined as the heavy's commander swung it around to line up with the roof. But before he could fire, Jennings's Griffin dove down out of the sky. "Heavy Three Eight," he radioed, reading the vehicle's number painted on the top plates. "This is Dragon One Four, I've got him."

Gunner had barely finished his transmission when Revell triggered a ten-round burst from the Chain gun. The Boa Hoa gunner saw the chopper bearing down on him and was racing for cover when the rounds cut him down.

The shattered Scorpion launcher dropped from nerve-less fingers as the Vietnamese crumpled to the roof.

"Three Eight," Jennings radioed. "This is One Four, problem's over. You're clear to move out now."

"This is Heavy Three Eight, copy. Thanks for the

assist."

"No sweat," the pilot replied. "We'll stay on station in case anyone else wants to take a pot shot at you."

The next customer showed up a hundred meters later and sprayed the armored car with automatic weapons fire. But this time, the heavy's commander took care of it himself with a short burst from the turret. When the bullet ridden body fell out onto the sidewalk, the driver casually engaged the clutch and the armored car slowly continued on down the street.

Following behind the heavies, Zoomie and the men of his Tac Platoon were doing what they did best again. Operating as five man teams, they swept through the buildings, clearing them so the Seattle PD search teams could move in and check them in detail. At first, the Tac Teams were unopposed, the little shops and apartments contained nothing dangerous. But when they entered the second block, the fun began.

Zumwald had just stepped into the circle of light from a street lamp when a burst of automatic fire sent him leaping for cover in a nearby doorway.

"Jesus!" he said softly as another burst chipped bricks right above his head.

"Five," he called to his sniper over the team radio net, "can you get that bastard?"

"Negative, One," the sniper answered. "Stay put. He's got this intersection covered. I'll see if I can find a firing position in the building behind you."

Zumwald didn't want to wait that long to get moving again. Switching over to the air operations frequency, he keyed the throat mike on his helmet. "Dragon One Zero, this is Tac One. I've got some business for you."

"One Zero, copy," Wolff answered. "Send it."

"We've got a sniper with a light machinegun in a top

126

floor window at the northeast corner of grid three. He's got us pinned down."

"One Zero, copy."

Less than a minute later, Zumwald heard the sound of a Griffin approaching. "Tac One, this is Dragon One Three, can you mark the target for me?"

"Copy," Zumwald called back. "Wait one." He stuck the barrel of his MP around the corner and fired a long burst at the top of the building.

As expected, the hidden Boa Hoa gunner took the bait and fired back at him.

"This is One Three," the Griffin's pilot radioed. "I've got him now. Stay down."

Holding in a hover, the gunship dropped down level with the top floor of the building. The sniper panicked when he saw the Griffin right in front of him. Unwisely, he opened up on the chopper with his light machinegun. Instantly, the Griffin's gunner answered the fire with a short burst from his grenade launcher.

Three rounds of 40mm HE shot in through the open window and detonated. A ball of flame shot out of the window. Shards of glass and chunks of shattered brick showered down onto the sidewalk.

"That should take care of him, Tac One," One Three radioed. "But I'll stick around just in case he has some friends."

"This is Tac One, thanks."

"No problem."

With the chopper hovering protectively overhead, Zumwald stepped out of his doorway. "Cover me," he radioed as he took off across the street.

Ducking back into cover on the other side of the street, he waved the rest of his team on across. Protected by the hovering gunship, they too made it across unmolested.

"Okay, boys," he radioed his team. "Let's flush this

thing out."

Moving out like they were back at the TPF training base, the five man Tac Team started clearing the bottom floor. As had happened in the other buildings they had swept, the inhabitants willingly opened their doors and allowed their small apartments to be quickly searched.

As soon as the bottom floor was secured, the Tac Team started up the stairs to clear the next floor and the Seattle police moved in behind them to do a detailed search. Everything went smoothly until they reached the top floor.

Zoomie led the assault up the stairs. He stopped behind the corner of the stairwell and took a flash-bang grenade from his harness. Pulling the pin, he rolled the grenade out into the hall. Five seconds later, it detonated.

Covered by the explosion, he lunged out from behind the cover, his MP-5 at the ready. The hall was clear. His backup man stepped out with him, his finger on the trigger of his automatic shotgun. Zumwald pointed down the hall. The shotgunner nodded and slowly started walking forward, his eyes darting from side to side checking the closed doors of the apartments. Behind them, the other three team members waited silently in the stairwell until the two point men got a little farther down the hall.

The shotgunner on point was in mid-stride when one of the doors swung open behind him. Whirling around, he went into a crouch and brought the muzzle of the shotgun to bear on the doorway. His finger was tightening down on the trigger, when he saw that his target was an old man.

"Get back inside!" he said harshly, jerking the muzzle aside.

"The bad men are there," the old man whispered,

pointing a shaking finger at a door on the opposite side of the hallway.

"Okay," the cop said softly. "Now, please get back inside!"

Zumwald joined the shotgunner and motioned for the other three men of the team to move up the hall so they could support them when they went through the door. The minute they were in place, Zumwald readied a grenade and signaled the shotgunner to go ahead. Two blasts of the 12 gauge sent the door flying off its hinges. A muffled scream was heard inside the room as the door went down with a crash.

Without exposing himself, Zumwald tossed the flash-bang grenade in as far as he could. When it went off, he and the shotgunner stormed into the apartment. A solitary figure darted into a side room and slammed the door behind him. Two more shotgun blasts opened that door too, and the fugitive came racing out, the AK-94 in his hands spitting fire.

Zumwald opened up with his MP-5 an instant before a final shotgun blast blew the man back into the room. He was dead before he hit the floor.

The room was quickly searched and, except for the sniper who had been killed by the gunship and the man Zumwald and the shotgunner had killed, the only Boa Hoa left was the wounded man lying under the front door.

The team quickly checked the rest of the floor and found that it was clear. A quick call on the radio got the medics upstairs to treat their wounded prisoner, and the Seattle police to take him into custody.

Zumwald peered around the corner of the building as he listened to the reports from his other three assault teams. This was the last block to be cleared and it didn't look like it would be any different from any of the others they had worked their way through. Just one more three-story brick building, piece of cake. He glanced down at his watch; they'd be done with this before the club closed for the night.

He waited until the other teams and their heavies were in position before he gave the word to move out. "All Tac units, this is Tac One," he radioed. "Let's do it. Tac Three, you go for the lower floors. We'll cover you."

Tac Three's heavy broke cover and slowly moved out into the intersection at the northwest corner of the block, its turret slowly sweeping the dark, empty windows. The heavy patrol car didn't make it more than ten feet before a Scorpion anti-tank rocket hit the right side of its front plate.

The jet of super heated gas from the exploding shaped-charge warhead punched through the armor and spread destruction inside the vehicle. A ball of flame blew open the rear doors and shot out of the command turret hatch.

Two of the three crewmen managed to get out of the inferno. The systems operator, however, didn't make it. The jet of gas and molten metal had cut right through him, fusing his flesh to his commo gear.

The sound of the rocket explosion was still echoing down the street when the entire upper floor of the building erupted with automatic weapons fire. Almost every window spouted flickering red orange flame.

"Take cover!" Zumwald yelled over the radio as he dove back around the corner.

From their orbit high in the sky, Rick Wolff and Mugabe had watched the battle rage in the streets below. They could see the barricades the Seattle police

130

had erected to keep the citizens away from the combat zone, but they could see that a huge crowd had gathered nonetheless. This was the best show in town, a full fledged shootout in the streets with helicopter gunships hovering overhead.

And so far, the other three Griffins were doing quite nicely on their own and there had been no call for One Zero's services as a gunship. Wolff and Mugabe had had to sit tight in their orbit and play C and C ship while everyone else had had all the fun.

So far, there had been no signs of the Viper missiles. All the choppers had encountered so far was some automatic weapons fire and, not even heavy caliber stuff at that, just light weapons. For some reason, Dong was holding his anti-aircraft missiles back and the armored Griffins had wiped out their opposition without taking a scratch. But Wolff wasn't about to complain.

As they watched, the news came in over the radio that the ground forces had cleared another block. Wolff checked the map on his tactical screen and coded that block as cleared. It looked like the only block left to be searched was one that held a large brick building.

Suddenly, a ball of flame erupted from an intersection below; one of the heavies had blown up. He could barely make out the tiny figures of the crew abandoning the vehicle and running from the flames. The men had barely reached cover when the front of the building they had been approaching erupted in fire.

The Tac channel burst into life as all of the Tac Teams tried to transmit at once. It was complete chaos, but Wolff was able to make out that the building was some kind of strong point. They had finally found the heart of the Boa Hoa.

"Let's hit it, Mojo," Wolff grinned, as he dropped the nose of his gunship. They were going to get a chance to play tonight after all.

"All Dragon ships," he radioed as his chopper dove out of the night sky. "This is One Zero, form up on me. We'll come in from the north side, and run a race track until Zoomie can get his people under cover. Then we'll do a little close air support work. How copy?"

The other three ships radioed their acknowledgement as they got in line behind Wolff's Griffin. "Tac One," Wolff radioed to Zumwald. "This is Dragon One Zero. Any time you're ready."

"Tac One, copy. Go now!"

Wolff led the gunships down out of the night sky. In the left seat, Mugabe centered his helmet visor sight in the upper story window on the far right, watching the glowing red range numbers flick past at the top of the sight picture. When the range read 500 meters, he pressed down on the trigger to the Chain gun.

The Griffin's airframe shuddered under the recoil of the heavy 25mm cannon as he walked his fire from right to left, sweeping the line of top story windows.

The 25mm HE shells blew big chunks out of the brick facing of the building, but could not penetrate the concrete inner walls. It would have taken a tank's armor-piercing rounds to punch through them. They could, however, make it damned uncomfortable for anyone trying to fire out of the windows.

There was scattered return fire from the building, but it was all light caliber. The few rounds that hit the chopper, ricocheted off the ship's armored skin and Lexan canopy. Mugabe kept firing till the last possible moment as Wolff banked away over the roof to clear the line of fire for Jennings.

Revell made her firing run using her 40mm grenade launcher. Most of the deadly grenades flew in through the windows and detonated inside. The flashes of the explosions revealed glimpses of the interior as if illuminated with a red strobe light. She could see men frantically scrambling to get away from the bombs.

Under the covering fire of the choppers, two of Zumwald's Tac Teams ran across the street and took cover against the base of the wall. As soon as they were in place, Zoomie led his team across himself. With the other two teams providing fire support, they would storm the bottom floor and start working their way up to the top.

When everyone was in place, Zumwald keyed his mike. "Okay, boys, let's do it!"

CHAPTER 17

"Little Saigon"

Zoomie and his men hurled grenades in through a shattered ground floor window and stormed in after the explosions. Quick, well-aimed bursts of fire cut down the few Boa Hoa in front of them. They quickly secured and fanned out to search for more of the gang.

Behind them, another of Zumwald's teams entered through another window and they soon cleared the ground floor. A stairwell in the back of the building led up to the apartments on the second floor. According to the Seattle PD, the apartments were occupied by civilians so they would have to be extremely careful.

Zumwald led the way up the stairs himself. The hallway between the apartments was deserted and, at the end of the hall was a fire door that led to the stairwell leading up to the top floor. It didn't take a military genius to realize that the stairwell would be defended.

He quickly brought another of his teams up to cover the stairwell while he evacuated the people living in the apartments. If they were going to have to fight their way up stairs, he didn't want a bunch of innocent civilians getting killed.

As soon as the floor was empty, he gave the order for Tac Two to try the stairs. The first man through the door was greeted with a burst of AK fire.

The leader of the Red Fist Commandos, Captain

Minh, looked around the smoke-filled upper floor of the building. The concentrated fire from the choppers made it impossible for his men to shoot out of the windows and most of them had moved down to where the battle was raging to hold the stairwell leading up to the top floor.

As far as Minh was concerned, the battle had gone well. He would have liked to stay and fight a little longer, but he knew that it was imperative that they leave before any of the men in the building were captured by the police. The colonel had been quite emphatic about that. With the police now in the lower floors of the building, every second they stayed meant that there was a greater chance that someone would fall into their hands alive.

He didn't have to worry about the fighters who had been out in the streets. They were throwaways, men who knew nothing about Dong's island or the nuke warhead. If they were captured, the police would learn nothing from them. The fighters in the building, however, were the cream of the Red Fist Commandos. They knew the details of the entire operation and could not be allowed to fall into the enemy's hands.

It was time to pull out, and that meant he had to see to his dead and wounded fighters. The dead were no problem, a quick shot to the head insured that they remained dead. But he had to check on his wounded.

The first man was on his feet, tying a bandage around his upper arm. "Wait at the elevator," Minh told the man.

"Can you walk?" Minh asked the next man who had a bloody bandage wrapped around his thigh.

"I don't know," the commando answered through gritted teeth. "I think my leg is broken."

Minh made a quick decision. If this fighter didn't know if he could walk, than he probably couldn't and

135

Minh didn't have time to have him carried out. Not through the tunnels under the building.

The Red Fist commander drew a thin stiletto from the sheath of his boot top. Distracting the wounded man for an instant, he stabbed the razor-sharp blade into the side of his neck right under the ear, severing the carotid artery. The man fell back and Minh turned to the second man.

He didn't have to ask if this one could make it by himself. He was dying of a bad chest wound and Minh merely hastened the process. He wiped the blade clean on the man's uniform before resheathing it in his boot top.

"Pull back!" he shouted over the roar of gunfire. "Pull back!"

The surviving fighters abandoned their firing positions and ran for the big elevator in the center of the floor. When they had all crowded into it, Minh punched the button for the bottom floor. The doors slid shut and a second later, they were on their way to the protected lower level and their escape route away from the building.

When the elevator reached the bottom floor, Minh waited while the other men got out. Before he stepped out, he opened the plate under the switch panel and using his security card, initiated the auto-destruct sequence. In sixty seconds, the explosive charge on the elevator machinery would detonate leaving the elevator on the bottom floor and blocking the shaft with debris. There was no stairwell leading down to the bottom floor, not even a fire escape. No one would be able to enter that level until the elevator was repaired. He had just locked the police away from their escape route.

Letting the doors slide shut behind him, Minh sprinted for the hidden exit at the other end of the room. Behind the door was a short tunnel that led into the famous Seattle Underground and their escape route.

After the disastrous fire of 1889, downtown Seattle had been completely leveled. The ground level had been raised several feet and new structures had been built on top of the fill. In later years, some of the fill had been excavated revealing the still standing basements of the older buildings. Tunnels had been cut joining them together in a maze and the Seattle Underground was born. At one time, the Underground had been one of Seattle's biggest tourist attractions. Thousand of visitors had toured the 19th century storefronts and sidewalks under the modern skyscrapers.

In 1999, however, no tourist or Seattle citizen in his or her right mind would dare go into the subterranean maze. Not even the police went down there except in force. It was a completely lawless haven for only the most desperate criminals and crazed druggies. It was worth a man's life to be caught in the Underground. But as well armed as they were, Minh did not fear the inhabitants. If they gave him any trouble, he would simply blow them away like the scum they were.

"Hurry!" Minh ordered.

Even though the police couldn't follow them through the Underground, he wanted to get to their rendezvous point as fast as he could so he could rejoin his leader on the island fortress.

On the second floor, Zumwald felt the building shake when the elevator exploded. He stopped for a moment when he realized that there was no fire coming from the upper floor of the building. "Tac Two!" he radioed to the team trying to break through the second door at the top of the stairwell. "Report!"

"One, this is Two," the team leader radioed back. "They've pulled out!"

137

"You sure?"

"Wait one, we'll blow the door."

A few seconds later, a muffled explosion sounded from the stairwell. The team had sent for a miniature shaped charge to blow through the door lock and it had done its job. The men of Tac Team Two stormed through the blasted door.

"It looks clear," Tac Two radioed.

"Check it out and get back to me ASAP."

"Two copy."

A few minutes later, Tac Two reported that the top floor was deserted and Zumwald got on the horn back to Buzz in the Motac. "It's all over," he radioed. "They've gone. I think they took an elevator down to a hidden basement. There's an elevator shaft up here, but it's been destroyed."

"Search the entire building before you stand down," Buzz ordered. "Make sure they didn't leave any men behind."

"Tac One, copy."

Now that the party was over, Wolff sent two of the Griffins back to the base, but he kept Jennings with him in case everyone hadn't gotten the word that the battle had ended. While Zumwald's men searched the building, the two choppers continued to fly low orbits over the structure.

Nguyen Thich Le clutched the Red Chinese AK-94 assault rifle in his hands as he huddled at the bottom of the concrete airshaft in the building next to Dong's old headquarters. Leaning against the side of the cement wall was a stolen Army Scorpion anti-tank rocket launcher. His orders had been to fire on any of the armored cars that he saw below him, but the battle had erupted so fast that he had not had a chance to use it.

Le was only sixteen and, not only was this his first mission for the Boa Hoa, it had been his first gun battle. When the fight broke out, instead of shooting his weapons when he had the chance, he had frozen in fear at the bottom of the airshaft. Now it seemed that the battle was over. At least, all was quiet now.

He raised his head over the edge of the well and looked down at the street below. Camouflage uniformed police swarmed over the headquarters building across the street. Other police, in blue uniforms and riot gear, led civilians away from the building under the protective guns of armored cars.

Le ducked back down before he could be spotted. He thought about trying to shoot at one of the armored cars down on the street. But to get a good shot at it, he would have to leave the safety of the air shaft and go over to the edge of the roof. The young would-be gangster, however, was afraid to do that. He wanted to do something to prove his bravery, but if the police were strong enough to drive the Red Fist fighters away, they would surely see him and kill him too.

At that moment, a huge shiny helicopter flew low over his head, the sudden blast of air from its rotors startled him. Le ducked back down in fear. But as the chopper passed just a few meters over the rooftop, he realized that he could shoot at it without having to leave his position. If the Scorpion missile would destroy an armored car, it would certainly take care of a helicopter. Colonel Dong would certainly approve of that and accept him into his ranks.

He quickly readied the Scorpion launcher for firing and waited for the chopper to return again. When it did, he would shoot at it and then make his escape.

Gunner Jennings flew a low orbit over the remains of

139

Dong's headquarters. Now that the shooting was over, he was ready to go back to the barn and call it a night. With nothing left to shoot at, he was getting bored. In the left seat of the Griffin, Sandra Revell kept an eye out on the buildings below.

For the last three hours, she had been at the controls of the chopper's sensors and weapons systems and, now that the long battle was over, she wasn't as alert as she had been at the beginning. The adrenaline rush was over and she was tired.

Had Sandra been a little more alert, she might have noticed the moving shadow in the air vent shaft of the building they were approaching. And, had she noticed it, she would have flicked on the low light optics to take a better look at the shadow.

But with all the street lighting below, she had not needed to use the low light optics to track her targets and they had been turned off since the beginning of the mission. Therefore, she missed seeing the young Vietnamese raise the Scorpion launcher to his shoulder and sight in on their low, slow flying chopper.

All she saw was the flash as the anti-tank rocket left the launching tube.

A thundering explosion rocked the Griffin, slamming her forward against her shoulder harness. The shaped-charge warhead punched through the outer skin on the belly of the ship. Fragments ripped into the fuel tanks as the main charge continued on up to destroy the rotor gearbox.

Dragon One Four staggered in the air for a moment and then plummeted to the ground.

Wolff saw the Scorpion hit Jennings' Griffin. The explosion engulfed the belly of the ship. "Oh Christ!"

"Gunner!" he shouted over the radio. There was no reply as the wounded Griffin crashed onto the rooftop of the building below. The machine hit hard, collapsing the landing skids and sending it smashing into the retaining wall at the edge of the flat roof. It rolled halfway over onto its side and the still spinning rotor blades hit the roof and splintered, sending fragments spinning through the air.

Wolff dove down and went into a hover over the rooftop. He was looking for a place to set down when sparks from the damaged ship's electronics bay ignited the leaking JP-4 from the ruptured fuel tanks. The Griffin was engulfed in a ball of flame.

"Gunner! Legs! You're on fire!" Wolff yelled over the radio. "Get out of there!"

He could see the figures in the cockpit struggling to undo their shoulder harnesses as the flames licked at the cockpit doors. Maneuvering his ship down as low as he could take it, Wolff pulled in full pitch and aimed the down blast of the rotors at the inferno.

The hurricane-like blast of air blew the fire away from the cockpit. "Get out of there!" Wolff radioed again.

Le was outraged when he saw Wolff's Griffin sweep down to rescue the cops in the first chopper. He had shot them down and he would not let them get away. He snapped his assault rifle up to his shoulder. Carefully sighting across the roof at the figures in the cockpit of the second ship, he triggered off a long burst of automatic fire.

Mugabe was so engrossed in watching Jennings and Revell struggle to get out of their burning machine, he missed seeing the young Vietnamese raise up from behind the air shaft bent to his left. The sudden burst of AK fire ricocheting off his side window, however, quickly got his attention.

The gunner snapped his head around to focus in on the shadowy figure. Slaved to his helmet controls, the

Griffin's nose turret followed Mugabe's line of sight. When the cross hairs in his face shield were centered on the muzzle blast of the AK, he triggered his Chain gun.

The short burst of 25mm cannon shells blew Le away along with much of the thin concrete air shaft wall. He flipped to low light optics and quickly scanned their surroundings to make sure that there were no more unfriendlies who wanted to play stupid games. There were none.

By this time, Gunner had freed himself and was pulling Sandra from the wreckage. "Set it down!" Mugabe shouted, reaching for his own harness release.

Wolff dropped down onto the roof and Mugabe jumped out of the cockpit and raced for the burning ship. Jennings and Revell had gotten out of the cockpit, but were still endangered by the fire. Mugabe scooped Sandra up in his arms and, with Gunner running along beside him, sprinted for Dragon One Zero.

He slid open the side door, boosted Sandra up into the rear compartment and helped Gunner aboard. He quickly strapped them in and slid the door shut. "Go! Go! Go!" he shouted up to the pilot.

Wolff hit full throttle and hauled up on the collective, pulling maximum pitch to the rotor blades. The ship leaped up into the air and he threw it into a hard bank. The medical facility at the Coast Guard base was the closest hospital and he could be there in three minutes.

"How're they doing?" he called back.

"They're okay!" Mugabe shouted. "They're just shook up. You can slow this son-of-a-bitch down now so you don't kill us all rushing to the hospital."

Wolff laughed and throttled back a little. "Copy, I'll have the medics standing by anyway."

142

CHAPTER 18

TPF Tactical Operations Center

A cold, drizzly morning broke over The Puget Sound. Indian summer had ended and the rain had returned to Seattle. For the next four months, the sun would rarely be seen in this corner of the Pacific Northwest. Somehow, the dark skies suited the scene in "Little Saigon."

Several blocks around Dong's building had been devastated in the battle. Apartments and shops had been destroyed and people were searching through the ruins for anything that remained of their possessions. Well-armed Seattle police were patrolling the area to prevent looting and to guard against any Boa Hoa members who still wanted to fight. The weapons were not needed, however, the Boa Hoa were gone and life in "Little Saigon" was quiet.

This did not mean, however, that life in the Asian enclave would ever be exactly the same as it had been. For the last ten years, the Vietnamese gang had completely dominated everything that had happened in the area. Now there was a power vacuum in the Asian community of "Little Saigon." The residents knew that it wouldn't last very long.

The weary Griffin flight crews sat in the corner of the Coast Guard mess hall and ate an early breakfast. "It's nice to see that the military hasn't forgotten how to make SOS," Mugabe said as he wolfed down a plate full of chipped beef on toast.

Wolff shuddered. Just the thought of eating anything that looked like that was enough to put him off his feed for days. His experience with SOS when he had been a cadet at the Air Force Academy had scarred him for life. "How can you eat that crap?" he asked his copilot.

"It's easy, my man," Mugabe answered. "You just open your mouth and . . ."

"As soon as you two quit jacking off," Red's voice broke in. "I expect to see your young asses out on the flight line. You got the hell shot out of your ship again and we've got a lot of work to do before she's going to be ready to fly again."

"Red!" Wolff said, looking up. "I didn't see you come in. Grab a cup of coffee and have a seat. Mojo here was just about to tell me all about the joys of eating SOS. I'm sure you'll want to hear all about it."

Red looked disgusted. Like Wolff, military breakfasts were not very high on his list of favorite things. "All I want to hear about this morning is two chopper cops helping me put their bird back together."

"But, Red," Wolff smiled. "We didn't do anything wrong this time, we were just trying to help Gunner and Legs out of a bind."

"I know," the maintenance chief said, pulling a fresh cigar from the pocket of his coveralls. "That's the only reason that you two hot shots aren't singing soprano this morning."

He bit the end off the cigar, stuck it in his mouth and fired it up. "And I will have a cup of coffee before I escort you to the flight line."

Sandra Revell and Daryl Jennings walked up with their breakfast trays. Neither one of them looked like they had slept in days.

"Have a seat," Wolff waved his hand. "Join the parade."

Sandra turned pale.

"What's up, girl," Mugabe smiled at her. "Not feeling well?"

"Not feeling well?" Legs snapped. "If you don't shut your ugly face, you're not going to be 'feeling well' yourself."

"My, aren't we out of sorts today?"

"Knock it off, Mojo," Jennings said quietly.

Mugabe wisely shut up. When Gunner got defensive about his co-pilot, it was time to back off.

Wolff drained the last of his coffee and stood up. "Come on, Red, Mojo," he said. "We've got work to do."

Jennings watched the three walk out of the Coast Guard mess hall. "Someday," he growled. "I'm going to . . ."

"No," Sandra said. "Mojo didn't mean anything. He's just got this weird way of winding down. He always gets like that after a bad mission."

"How are you feeling?" he asked.

"I can't stop shaking," she said. "This stuff usually doesn't bother me, but that was just too damned close last night." Sandra hated to admit to him that she was still so shaken up. It went against her image as being as tough a cop as any of the men.

"Yes, it was," Jennings agreed.

"If it hadn't been for those two," she shuddered. "We'd both be . . ."

"I know," the pilot said quietly as he picked up his coffee cup. "I know."

Sandra cradled her coffee cup in both hands seeking comfort from the warmth as she stared out the window at the dark blue Griffin helicopters sitting on the ramp outside. In the cold, wet dawn they looked like crouching prehistoric monsters. She shuddered and wondered if she'd ever feel comfortable flying in one of them again.

* * *

145

The raid on "Little Saigon" had not been a raging success as far as Buzz Corcran was concerned. It was true that they had captured quite a few weapons and had rounded up some two dozen suspects, both Boa Hoa and common run-of-the-mill maggots. And, most importantly, they had brought that part of Seattle back under effective control of the local government. That was the up side.

In the negative column, they hadn't found anything that gave them a lead to the whereabouts of the Trident missile warhead and they hadn't caught the infamous Colonel Dong. Also, they hadn't found a trace of Lieutenant Tran; the CO of the Seattle TPF field office was still missing. Buzz had no facts to back it up, but he was certain that Dong had a hand in that mystery as well.

The worst part of all, however, was that for so little gain, the Tac Force had had one man killed, three more wounded, one heavy patrol vehicle destroyed and one Griffin helicopter badly damaged. As far as he was concerned, it had not been a good trade off.

Buzz scanned the after-action report again, looking for anything he might have missed on the first reading, but it didn't get any better the second time around. He knew that he still had to wait for the interrogation of the suspects they had taken into custody at the Space Needle to be completed before he would have the entire picture. But the preliminary information he had been given so far wasn't telling him much of anything.

The Tactical Police Act gave the TPF the authority to use chemical interrogation on suspects involved in terrorist acts if doing so would provide information to save lives. The evidence gathered that way could not be used against the suspect in court, but that usually didn't matter. In terrorist incidents, saving lives was the top prior-

146

ity. To use the chemicals required getting clearance all the way from Washington and it was rarely given. But in this case, Buzz hadn't even had to ask to use them. The TPF Headquarters had sent him orders to put anyone he caught under the needle immediately.

It usually took twenty-four hours for the chemical interrogation to run its course, but useful information was usually available by the second hour that the drugs were working on the suspect. So far, though, it looked like none of the people they had nabbed knew anything about anything. Least of all, anything about that damned warhead.

Either an entirely different bunch of Dinks had hijacked the warhead or the Boa Hoa leader was being extremely careful about who he shared his information with. Even the people within his own ranks. Buzz hated to admit it, but it looked like the ball was still in Dong's court and they were back to square one with no leads.

Corcran was disappointed with the sweep, but Mayor Johnson had turned the Tac Force operation into a media event to promote his administration. The morning papers and TV news were full of photos of the mayor proudly displaying the weapons that had been captured last night. In his statements to the press, he smugly took credit for having had the foresight to call in the feds to "assist" the Seattle PD with the pacification of "unruly elements" in "Little Saigon."

Buzz didn't even bother wasting his time getting pissed at this misrepresentation of the facts, he was used to local politicos taking credit for the TPF's work. It made his job more difficult, but it was a fact of life. At least the fool hadn't leaked anything to the press about the missing warhead. The secret was still safe, for now.

That hadn't taken any of the pressure off him, however. The Denver Regional Headquarters was still on the phone every hour requesting updates on the status of the missing nuke and they were not going to like the fact that the interrogation was yielding nothing.

Part of the reason that Denver had so readily agreed to let him invoke the Tactical Police Force Act was that he had convinced them that he could recover the warhead in the sweep. Or at least obtain hard information about it. But now, his job was on the line again as the politicians in Washington lined up to second guess his handling of the situation.

Buzz was also used to this part of his job. According to Denver, there already were congressional demands that the Tac Force be pulled out of Seattle and the CIA be sent in to find the missile. As far as he was concerned, that was just another example of political dumb thinking coming out of Washington. Spooks never accomplished anything.

Part of Buzz's problem, though, was that with Lieutenant Tran missing, the Seattle field office was in an uproar. Usually Buzz could depend on the local TPF field offices to provide Dragon Flight with an intelligence network already in place and knowledgeable about the local situation. This time, however, the field office was striking out in a big way. Too much of their intelligence operation depended on Lieutenant Tran. Without him, the support office effectively shut down.

Corcran vowed that as soon as he got his hands on that young cop, he was going to tear him to ribbons. A field office commander's place was behind his desk, not out hitting the bricks like some first year rookie.

The only good news this morning was that Denver was airlifting him a new Griffin to replace the one he had lost the night before. Also, they were finally sending the neutrino detectors that would let them search for the nuke from the air and technicians to install it on his choppers. Maybe there was still a chance that they could salvage something from this mess before some congress-

148

man blew the whistle.

The Tac Force commander looked at the large scale map of the Greater Seattle area and the surrounding counties. He was sure that wherever that missile had been taken, it hadn't been moved very far. If Dong had intended to take it somewhere else, he wouldn't have brought it into Seattle in the first place. The question was, where had he taken it?

Buzz knew that the answer to that question was tied up with what Dong intended to do with it. And that was the critical question that no one had an answer to.

So far, the Tac Force had been running around frantically trying to find the damned thing and very little thought had been given to why it had been hijacked in the first place. There was something about having eight nukes running around loose that made people extremely nervous.

Buzz poured himself another cup of coffee and returned to the map. There were only so many things that could be done with a warhead like that. For one, Dong could have stolen it to sell to a foreign power. That was likely. In that case, it was probably on its way to a pick up point—either by air or sea. The second thing he could do with the eight MIRVs in the warhead was to use them for blackmail purposes. It was relatively easy to do and it fit with what he knew of Dong's history. Thirdly, he could use the warhead as it had been intended, to wipe someplace off the map. That was probably the least likely of the three possibilities. Had the gang leader intended to do that, he would have stolen the rest of the missile so he could launch it, not just the warhead itself.

It was high time that he got this operation back on track. Someone had to make a decision and that's what the government paid him to do. He decided that Dong was going to use the nukes for blackmail; the only question was what was he going to threaten them with, and where.

He turned to his desk and hit the button to his intercom. "Get Avila, Zumwald, Wolff and who the hell ever's running the field office in here ASAP."

"Yes, sir."

He turned back to the map and his eyes moved to the number of military bases and defense contractors in the Greater Seattle area. There was the nuclear sub base at Bangor, McCord Air Force Base, the Naval Air Station at Widby Island, the ship yards at Bremerton, Boeing's manufacturing facilities at Seattle and Renton. The Greater Seattle area was one of the most concentrated military complexes in the nation, and one of the most important.

Not only was the business community focused on the Pacific Rim, Asia was also the focus of the only real military threat to the nation. When the Soviet Union had given up her dreams of military conquest, Red China and her allies, North Korea and a revitalized Vietnam, had become the new international threat. Like the economic institutions in Greater Seattle, the military facilities in the area were also focused on the Pacific Rim, but on protecting it.

If Dong was going to use the warhead to threaten something in the Seattle area, what was a better target than one of the military bases?

CHAPTER 19

TPF Tactical Operations Center

Buzz and his officers were going over the situation in his office when the intercom on his desk buzzed. "Captain," Ruby said. "I've got a sergeant from the field office here who says that he has to see you ASAP."

"Send him on in."

The door opened and Sergeant Sunami, the field office operations sergeant, walked in. "We've finally got something for you, sir," he said.

"You find your lieutenant yet?"

"No, sir," Sunami frowned. "We've searched everywhere and talked to all of his contacts. But no one has seen him."

"Shit!" Buzz said. "Okay, let's have your news."

"We finally got somewhere with the interrogation of the guys we took into custody at the Space Needle," the sergeant said. "But I don't know what it means."

"What do you have?"

"One of the suspects just gave us a rundown on his military training in North Korea."

"North Korea?" Buzz frowned.

"Yes, sir," Sunami continued. "He said that he was trained at a place right outside of Pyongyang. The North Korean Special Forces school."

"What in the hell is Dong doing tied up with those guys?" Buzz asked rhetorically.

"Maybe he's going to give them the missile?" Avila suggested.

151

In the aftermath of the Fifth Arab-Israeli War in 1992, the North Koreans had replaced the Libyans as the main promoter and supplier of worldwide international terrorism. Qaddafi was radioactive dust in the ruins of Tripoli, but his spirit lived on in North Korea. Buzz shuddered to think what those bloodthirsty bastards would do if they got their hands on a nuclear missile. As far as he knew, not even the Red Chinese were crazy enough to trust the North Koreans with nuclear weapons.

"Is that all?" he asked the sergeant.

"No," Sunami paused. "There was something else about an island. We're still working on the details."

"What are you getting from the others?"

"Not a word," Sunami shook his head. "This is the only one who's broken yet."

"Keep on him," Buzz ordered. "And call me the minute you get anything more. Even one word."

"Yes, sir."

As soon as the sergeant left, Buzz reached for the secure phone on his desk. Denver would want to know about this tie-in with the North Koreans ASAP. The heat from Washington was getting serious and maybe this first hard lead would cool things down for a little while.

He was also hoping that their computer wizards could put something together regarding the North Koreans and an island. They were always bragging about how good they were at putting bits and pieces of information together. Now they could prove to him just how good they were by solving this puzzle.

He knew that it was a real long shot, but he thought that it was worth a try. They sure as hell weren't getting anywhere with it on their own.

"Ruby," he said. "Patch me into Denver."

Red had his full maintenance crew waiting on the runway when the big C-9 transport landed at the Coast Guard base. The plane had barely turned off her jet engines when Red lowered the ramp door down and started supervising the unloading of the replacement helicopter. With the situation as up in the air as it was, he wanted the new machine checked out and ready to go as soon as possible.

In minutes, the Griffin was winched out of the cargo hold and towed over to the Tac Force ramp. As the powerplant mechanics climbed up to attach the main rotor blades, the sensor technicians and fire control people started unbuttoning the inspection panels to do their checks. Red waited around to see that they were doing it right before ducking into his office to look over the paperwork that had accompanied the new machine.

He started his third cigar of the day as he went over the log book, seeing what work had been done on the chopper over the last few months. For once it looked like he was in luck, Denver had sent him a ship that was in pretty decent shape this time. The last replacement he had gotten from depot maintenance had been a real piece of shit, but with any luck, he would be able to have this one sitting on line ready to go before the day was out.

He reached for the phone on his desk to call Jennings and Revell to have them report to maintenance to help work on their new machine. If his boys were busting their butts on it, they might as well have some company. After all, it was their fault that their old ship had been so badly damaged. They should have known better than to fly into the path of an anti-tank rocket.

He shook his head. He was mad about having the chopper shot up, but he was still glad that no one had been hurt, particularly Legs. He would not have liked to see her killed or maimed.

Like the other men in the Tac Force, Red had long ago reconciled himself to the idea of working with women cops. But, he would never get used to the feelings he had each time one of them got hurt. It was a tragedy when any cop was killed, but when one of the women was hurt, it hit something deep inside him, the old fashioned belief that men were supposed to gladly put their lives on the line and that women were to be protected from danger at all cost.

He knew that he had an antique viewpoint, but that was the way he looked at the world. He did try, however, to make sure that he kept his feelings to himself. After all, this was 1999, not the 1980's.

The maintenace chief placed his call and he was still going through the new chopper's log book item by item when Gunner Jennings poked his head into his office.

"Where's Legs?" Red growled when he saw that Gunner's co-pilot wasn't with him.

"She went on sick call right after breakfast," the pilot said.

"What's wrong with her?"

"She said she had a real bad headache," he shrugged. "Probably got shook up in the crash."

"Right!" Red's sympathy for women cops swiftly vanished when he realized that he didn't have anyone to do her work today. He thought for a moment.

"Go get Mojo," he said. "And get started on your hand-over check list ASAP. I want to get that damned thing on the line today."

"Wolfman's not going to like that."

"Fuck Wolff!" Red growled. "He gives you any static, you tell him to see me about it."

"You got it, Chief," Jennings grinned. He loved it when Red got on Wolff's case.

Out on the flight line, Wolff and Mugabe were doing

routine maintenance on their machine. The damage they had suffered last night had proven to be superficial. But even through nothing of any importance had been hit, there were still the daily checks that had to be made.

"I hate to interrupt you boys when you're on your coffee break," Jennings said when he walked up. "But Red said that I could borrow Mojo to help me get my new ship on line."

"Where's Legs?" Wolff asked. "She's supposed to be doing that kind of shit."

"She's feeling a little under the weather and checked in the sick bay."

"What's the matter with her?"

Jennings shrugged. "Don't know, but I think she's still pretty shook up."

"It can't have been the SOS for breakfast this morning," Mugabe said with a smile. "She didn't have any."

Jennings briefly considered punching Mojo in the mouth, but he needed his help today, so he tabled that notion for now. Maybe later. "Anyhow, Mojo," he said. "Let's hit it. We've got a lot of work to do today."

"Lead on, my man," Mugabe said.

Wolff watched the two cops walk over to the maintenance bay that sheltered the new ship. Sandra hadn't looked good this morning. But he'd thought that she'd snap out of it, she always had before. He decided that he'd better keep an eye on her. As the Dragon Flight leader, he didn't need to have a gunner who was losing her guts.

"Buzz," Ruby called over the intercom, "you need to take a look at this fax from Denver. It looks like they've found something for us."

'Bout fucking time, Buzz thought as he walked out and took the three-sheet report from the tray. It looked like the computer boys in Denver had been working overtime to live up to their reputation as whiz kids. Every possible connection between the North Koreans and the West Coast was listed in chronological order in the report. As he scanned through it, he saw that several of the incidents had occurred in the Greater Seattle Area, and he concentrated on them.

About five years ago there had been a case where some classified high-tech manufacturing equipment had been stolen from the Boeing plant and an attempt was made to smuggle it out of the country by boat. The Coast Guard, however, had been alerted and had intercepted a North Korean trawler trying to flee back out into international waters. When ordered to stop, the ship's captain had scuttled his boat rather than have it boarded and searched.

The Navy, however, had been able to raise the hulk and recover the stolen equipment. A footnote mentioned that it was believed that the trawler had made a rendezvous with the smugglers to transfer the cargo at Gray's Island far out in The Puget Sound.

There were other incidents ranging from North Korean agents captured to more smuggling incidents. But in the almost two dozen entries on the report, that was the only mention of an island, any island, anywhere.

Buzz picked up the phone and placed a call to the Coast Guard intelligence officer at the base. Yes, the man remembered the incident and yes, he could bring over the classified folder on it so Buzz could read through it.

A few minutes later, Ruby escorted the officer through the door. "Captain, Commander Rogers to see you."

"You got the file?" Buzz asked as he shook the officer's hand.

Rogers handed it over and Buzz started reading. "Just where is this Gray's Island?"

"Here," Rogers said, walking over to the map and pointing to a small land mass at the extreme western edge of The Puget Sound.

"What's there?" Buzz asked, looking at the map.

"Not much except for an abandoned federal prison right in the middle of it," the Coast Guard officer said.

"A prison?" Buzz frowned. "A prison?" What better place for a criminal to hide than in an abandoned prison? An out-of-the-way, massive concrete building that could hide a small army behind its walls.

"That's got to be it!" he said triumphantly, his finger stabbing the island on the map.

"It's certainly worth a look," the Coast Guard officer agreed.

Buzz punched the call button on his intercom. "Find Wolff and tell him to get in here ASAP," he said when Ruby answered.

A few minutes later, the pilot appeared at the door. "What's up, Captain?"

"I think we've finally got our first real lead," Buzz answered, his finger pointing to a speck on the map. "Gray's Island. There's an abandoned federal prison on it and, five years ago, a North Korean smuggling operation used it for a rendezvous point."

"What's the tie-in with North Korea?" Wolff asked.

Buzz realized that he had not yet briefed the Dragon Flight leader on the latest development. "It's a long story, but Dong's linked to them."

"Okay," Wolff said.

"How soon can you get that neutrino detector mounted on your ship and run a recon over that place?" Buzz asked.

The pilot glanced up at the clock on the wall. "With any luck at all," he said confidently. "We can get it done before dark."

"Good," Buzz nodded. "Do it."

"You got it, sir," the chopper cop said as he headed for the door.

Buzz turned back to his map. If his hunch was right and Dong was holed up in the old prison, he was going to need a little help clearing him out of there. That place was built like a regular fortress. He picked up his phone and started making calls.

CHAPTER 20

McCord Air Force Base

The young Air Police guard at the main gate to Mc-Cord Air Force base between Seattle and Tacoma glanced at the pass held up by the driver of the van and waved it on through. The sign on the side read "Happy Face Catering" and had the classic round yellow sun face wearing a smile painted on it. A young Oriental woman in the passenger seat of the cab smiled shyly as the truck drove away.

Without looking at his watch, the airman knew that it had to be within a minute of fourteen-thirty hours. For the last three months that he had been stationed at the main gate, the afternoon roach coach always came precisely at two-thirty, you could set your watch by it. One thing he could say for the young Asian refugee couple who ran that business, they took their work seriously. They were determined that they were not going to lose their contract to supply coffee, donuts and sandwiches to the hundreds of hungry workers at the sprawling airbase complex.

The previous vendor had had a real rotten attitude, but these guys were right on top of things. And, as an unexpected added bonus, their coffee was drinkable.

He always had a cup when the truck completed its rounds and was going back out the gate. Maybe he'd even get a donut today. When it was cold and drizzly, he always liked a fresh pastry. The van driver and his wife always seemed to hold back enough donuts and maple bars to take care of the Air Police detachment at the main gate at no charge.

Sure, it cost them a few bucks, but it was good for business.

The next truck was delivering office supplies. The guard made the driver get out and open the back of the truck before he would let it pass through. With all that was going on up in Seattle, the sergeant had told them to be extra careful about terrorists.

The Happy Face Catering van started its rounds of the hangars, flight lines and work shops as hundreds of airmen and civilian workers stopped for the afternoon coffee break. The roach coach made only one deviation from its normal rounds. At the back of the electronics warehouse building, the truck stopped close to the back door.

After glancing around to make sure that they were not being watched, the driver got out and undid a door leading into a secret compartment in the back of the van. Three men in black clothes quickly got out, pulling an Air Force blue box out behind them. While the driver kept watch, the men disappeared into the building taking the box with them.

After several minutes had passed, the three men in black emerged from the building without the box. They crawled back into the truck and the driver locked them back in the secret compartment. Climbing back into the cab, he continued on his rounds delivering his coffee and snacks. There were still a few stops to be made and everything had to look normal. Today of all days, he didn't need someone calling the main gate asking where he was.

The Air Police guard was not surprised that the roach coach was a little late coming back out. On a miserable day like this, more people would line up to get a cup of hot coffee. The truck pulled off into the turnout next to the gate and the Vietnamese couple came over to the guard house with a pot of coffee and a tray of pastries.

As he got his coffee cup filled and took a doughnut from the tray, he noticed that the young woman looked troubled by something. He almost asked her if something was wrong, but didn't. Probably, some loud mouth had made a pass at her or had called her a Dink. There was always some redneck asshole who seemed to delight in giving the Asian refugees a rough time.

He quickly drank his coffee and ate his donut. Stepping back out in the cold, he felt a little warmer. Only two and a half hours to go before he was off duty and could get out of the weather.

Tran was surprised when two of the Boa Hoa came and opened the door of his cell. Except for a man bringing him his meals, the police officer had been left in total isolation since he had been locked up.

"The colonel wants to see you," one of the guards said in Vietnamese. Tran walked into the corridor and the guards took up positions on either side of him. They led him into what must have been the watch commander's office on the ground floor. The outer office was filled with commo equipment consoles and surveillance camera screens and several Boa Hoa were manning them. Dong had isolated himself by coming to the island, but he was still in contact with his network.

Tran was led into an inner office where the colonel was obviously waiting for him. "Lieutenant Tran," Dong said, speaking English this time. "How nice to see you looking so well."

The gang leader turned to the man standing slightly behind him. "May I introduce Major Sung Kim of the People's Republic of Korea. Major, this is Lieutenant Phan Le Tran of the United States Tactical Police

161

Force."

Kim was a stocky, round-faced man wearing a khaki field uniform totally devoid of insignia. His hands and arms had the over-developed look of a martial arts devotee. Kim's round face was expressionless, but his dark eyes bored into the police officer like twin gun muzzles.

Tran bowed slightly and greeted Kim in Korean. Since his beat included such a large Asian population, he had learned the social niceties in most of the major Oriental languages spoken in Seattle. But if Kim was surprised to be greeted in his own tongue, there was no sign of it on his face. His black eyes still bored into him.

"The major has a few questions he wants to ask you," Dong explained.

"This Tactical Police of yours," Kim said in almost accentless English. "How many of them are there? How are they armed?"

Tran hesitated for a moment. His first thought was to say nothing. But he also had no illusions that this interrogation was going to be conducted without much regard to protecting his constitutional right to remain silent. If he didn't give the major the answers he wanted, they would simply be beaten out of him. And since he couldn't escape if he was beaten half to death, he decided to tell the Korean anything that he wanted to know. But he would also lie if he could get away with it.

"There are not very many of us," he answered honestly. "The Seattle field office has eighteen men."

"Are those the ones who fly the gunship helicopters?"

"No, the choppers are from Dragon Flight based in Denver," Tran answered. "My men do normal police work."

"How many helicopters?"

"Four."

"And how many police commandos? How do you call

them, SWAT Teams?"

"Twenty men." He didn't bother to mention that ten of his own people were Tac Team trained and could augment Zumwald's small force.

"So there are four gunships and twenty men."

"Yes."

The stocky Korean major stared at him for a long moment before abruptly spinning around on his heels and leaving the room.

"What's your connection with the North Koreans?" Tran asked as soon as Kim was gone. "Did they put you up to this crazy scheme?"

"You might say that we have been partners for years and we worked the plan out together."

"What's the purpose of all this?" Tran asked. "What in the hell are you going to do with eight atomic bombs?"

Dong smiled. "That's very simple. I am going to make the United States mind its own business for a change."

"What do you mean?"

"Since World War Two, your country has meddled in the affairs of the Far East, holding the fear of your nuclear arsenal over the heads of the great Asian leaders to force them to do your bidding."

Dong smiled. "But that is all ended now."

"What do you mean?"

"Now the threat is over your heads," Dong replied. "From now on, it is your government who will do the bidding of Asian leaders."

"What are you talking about? What Asian leaders?"

"Since 1954, your government has prevented the reunification of North and South Korea. They have supported a repressive capitalist regime in the south and have blocked all moves by the People's Republic to embrace their brothers in the South. Now, however, this long overdue reunion will finally take place."

"What in the hell are you talking about?" Tran shook

his head in disbelief. "The South Koreans don't want anything to do with the North. They're happy with their lives as the second greatest economic power in the Pacific Rim."

"They just think that they are happy," Dong said. "But when their brothers in the North show them the injustice of capitalism, they will embrace the simple life of the masses in the People's Republic."

"Aren't you forgetting that we have a treaty with the South?" Tran asked. "The minute the North Korean Army jumps the border, the entire United States military will go to the defense of South Korea."

"I don't think so," Dong's expression was gleeful. "Not if nuclear weapons are detonating under American military bases. Washington will think twice when they know that a nuclear firestorm will sweep the West Coast if they go to the aid of their puppet government in South Korea."

Tran was stunned. It was all so simple. Even one bomb exploding at a military base would throw the nation into shock, to say nothing of what would happen if all eight of the MIRVs in the Trident warhead were set off.

"Jesus! Thousands of innocent people including Asian refugees like yourself!"

"That is very unfortunate," Dong said. "But sadly, it is necessary to make a point. No longer will the United States dominate the affairs of the Far East. The first bomb was put into position this afternoon and the era of Yankee nuclear colonialism is finally over."

"But you can't do this," Tran said pointlessly.

"Obviously I can," the colonel pointed out with a smile. "And freedom loving peoples all over the world will applaud my actions. In just a few days, my name will go down in history along side those of Stalin, Mao and Ho Chi Minh as a powerful leader who has changed the world as we know it."

Tran shut up; he knew that there was no point in talking to this maniac any longer. He was frustrated. He was the only American who knew the danger the nation was facing and there was not a goddamned thing he could do about it.

The colonel called for the guards to return Tran to his cell. "I will tell you when the New Era breaks," Dong told the cop. "Though you will not rejoice, I am sure that you will want to know."

Tran just shook his head. He still could not believe that this was happening.

On the way back to his cell, Tran kept his eyes open for details of this prison. He was frantically looking for anything that might offer him an opportunity to get the hell out of this mess. But he knew it was in vain. Any maximum security federal prison was designed to thwart any attempts to escape and this place was no exception. Even though Dong wasn't using the full security precautions that had been built into the design, what he was using was sufficient.

Back in his cell, Tran was surprised to discover that he had a visitor. Or more properly, a cell mate. A young, thin, blond man wearing rumpled clothing sat slumped on the other bunk. He looked up when Tran was ushered into the cell.

"Who are you?" the man asked suspiciously.

"First, who are you?" Tran asked reverting back to being a cop.

"I'm Ralph Baker," the man answered automatically.

"What are you doing here?"

"Why should I tell you?"

"Because I may be able to help you," Tran answered. "I'm Lieutenant Phan Le Tran of the Tactical Police

Force."

That got the man's attention. "What in the hell are you doing here?"

"I fucked up," Tran answered honestly. "In a major way."

"Jesus," Baker put his head in his hands, "is he going to kill you too?"

"I don't know," Tran shrugged. "Why is he going to kill you?"

Baker looked up. "Because I'm the guy who fixed the bombs for him."

Tran stared at the man.

"I was a nuclear weapons technician on a missile sub," Baker went on to explain. "I'm AWOL from the Navy Boomer base at Bangor."

Tran vaguely remembered a report passing his desk several months ago about a missing nuclear missile tech. There had been a photograph attached to the report, but Tran had breezed over it and forgotten it. This was the missing piece of the puzzle that he could have used earlier. Had he remembered the report, he probably wouldn't have pulled the stupid stunt that had gotten him captured.

"Where is that warhead now?"

"It's here," Baker said. "At least most of it. One of the MIRVs has already been taken away."

"What do you mean?"

"Dong has been having me put remote controlled detonation devices on the MIRVs. I got the first one finished yesterday and they took it away."

"Do you know where they took it?"

"Not really, but it has to be somewhere close. The radio control I put on it only has a range of a hundred miles or so."

Tran's mind raced. That one bomb was probably still in the Seattle area. Probably planted at one of the local bases.

"Where are the rest of the bombs?"

"Down in the basement," Baker answered. "I finished them up today and when I told Dong, he had his goons throw me in here. He's going to kill me."

Tran didn't answer. This pitiful loser had made it possible for Dong to kill millions of people and now he was afraid that he was going to be one of them. It was a little late to be worrying about that now.

"He said that he would give me a million dollars," Baker continued, "and forget about my gambling debts. He also said that I could take one of the girls when I left. We were planning to go to somewhere in Latin America. Buy a ranch or something like that. He said . . ."

Tran sat down on his bunk and listened while Baker rambled on and on. This country was in danger and he was powerless to prevent it.

CHAPTER 21

Griffin Flight Line

Red furiously chomped on the end of his cigar as the sensor technicians hurried to finish installing the neutrino detector under the portside stub wing of Wolff's Griffin, Dragon One Zero.

"Are you sure that you don't want me to mount the 25mm for you?" he asked the pilot. "It won't take but a minute."

Wolff shook his head. "No thanks, Red. I've got too much extra gear hanging on her now. With the mission profile we're flying, I don't think I can take the extra weight. I'm gonna need all the speed and maneuverability I can get."

Wolff's Griffin had been turned in to a recon ship for the mission. Along with the neutrino detector under the port stubwing, he had a high speed recon camera pod under the starboard wing. Since they were flying into an air-to-air missile environment, the twin turbines had been fitted with the bulky "Black Hole" infrared suppression kits on the exhausts and an IRCM module in the top of the fuselage.

In theory, with the mirror skin turned up bright and the IR defenses working, they should be able to fly right through any kind of air defense system and have a good chance of coming out the other side unscratched. That was the theory, but the pilot still wanted to have his ship's maximum speed and maneuverability on call if he needed it. Even with all the fancy defenses, he knew that the best way to evade missiles was the use of a well-trained Mark 1 eyeball and a fast hand on the controls.

"I think we've got it, Chief," the technician reported to Red as he snapped the access plate back in place. "Have Mojo fire it up and see if it's working."

In the left seat of the Griffin, Mugabe activated the detector and watched the screen while one of the technicians stood in front of the chopper with a neutrino emitting device. The needle on the detector swung to the side and he heard a clicking noise in his earphones. He gave the technician a thumbs up and the man backed up farther and walked off to one side. Again the needle tracked the emitter; the detector was working.

Mugabe stuck his head out of the open window. "We're go," he told Wolff and Red.

The pilot tightened the Nomex gloves over his fingers and slipped his helmet down over his head. "Wish us luck," he said to Red as he opened the right side door and slid back the armored side of the pilot's seat to climb on board.

Red spat a piece of tobacco onto the tarmac. "You two be real careful out there," he said. "And you'd better not get this aircraft all fucked up either."

Wolff grinned as he buckled his shoulder harness straps. "We wouldn't do that to one of your babies, Red."

The maintenance chief didn't answer as he shut the pilot's door and made sure that it was latched. He had been sending chopper pilots off to do battle for years, but he had never quite gotten used to the feeling of helplessness it gave him. The nagging sense that there might have been something else he could have done to prepare the men for their ordeal was always there.

He stepped back and joined the other cops standing well clear of the rotors. Everyone who was not busy

169

with their duties had gathered to see Wolff and Mugabe off. They all knew what was hanging on this mission. If Wolfman and Mojo were successful and found the missing warhead, the Tac Force would all be heros. If they didn't, Washington was going to pull them out.

Wolff and Mugabe quickly ran through the takeoff check list and fired up the Griffin's twin GE turbines. As soon as the four-bladed rotor was spinning, Wolff clicked on the radio. "Dragon Control, this is Dragon One Zero, we're ready for takeoff.

"One Zero this is Dragon Control. You are clear to takeoff."

Cracking the throttle open as he gently hauled up on the collective, Wolff lifted the Griffin off the helipad in a low ground effect hover. He nudged down on the rudder pedal, swinging her tail around to line up with the runway. Twisting the throttle all the way up against the stop, he pushed forward on the cyclic control. The chopper's tail rose and she started down the runway in a classic gunship takeoff.

As soon as his airspeed came up, Wolff hauled up on the collective, pulling pitch on the rotor blades. The sleek, dark blue machine leapt up into the air.

As soon as the chopper cleared the shipping lanes around Seattle's harbors, Wolff brought his ship down right on the wave tops. Since there was also a good possibility that Dong had radar defenses as well as the Vipers, the plan was to make a low level, high speed approach to the island with the Griffin's skids kissing the wave tops all the way to stay under the radar horizon.

Then, when they reached the island, Wolff would go up to tree top altitude, make one fast pass over the deserted prison, every sensor turned up full blast, and make their escape as quickly as they could.

It sounded real good on paper, but both men knew that there was still a very good chance that they would be blown right out of the sky. All it would take would be one lookout on the beach with a Viper missile hot and running and their entire program would be null and void.

"Go full defensive now, Mojo," Wolff ordered.

Mugabe's fingers flew over his switches and controls and the outside skin of the Griffin turned bright chrome blue. The attack screen lit up with the data readouts from the full array of sensors. Everything from full spectrum radar to laser was being monitored.

"All systems go," Mugabe reported. "Sensors on full alert." His fingers hit the switches to the nose turret and dialed in his ammo selection, all HE. "Weapons hot."

"Copy," Wolff responded, his eyes scanning the navigational readout and the horizon.

A half hour later, a dark smudge appeared on the horizon in front of the Griffin. Wolff was flying so low that it was impossible for them to get an aerial perspective of the size of the island. The map on the navigational screen, however, showed that the deserted prison was situated exactly in the center of the land mass.

"Show time, Mojo," Wolff said as he lined the nose of the Griffin up on the center of the smudge.

"Copy," the systems operator answered curtly. With his eyes on his sensor readings, one hand wrapped around the weapons controls and the other poised by the decoy flare launch button, Mugabe had no time to get into a long conversation. At their present speed of 275 miles an hour, they would be over the target for only a few seconds. It would be a short exposure, but it was still time enough for a Viper gunner to get a lock-on and he had to be ready for it.

The rocky shelf of beach suddenly appeared in their windscreen, Wolff gently nudged the ship's nose up to clear the spindly fir trees ringing the beach. Now the perimeter fence and dull, gray walls of the prison were in sight. Wolff fed in a little rudder pedal to line up exactly with the center of the prison. He felt his heart racing and his hands tightened on the controls. "Here we go!"

Seconds later, they flashed past only meters above the roof top. "I've got a reading!" Mugabe shouted triumphantly. "Get us the hell outa here, Wolfman!"

"Roger that," the pilot said, his eyes locked on the airspeed indicator. "We're rolling."

Keeping the belly of the ship as close to the tops of the skinny fir trees as he could, Wolff's right hand unconsciously twisted the throttle even harder against the stop. The RPM governor was switched to increase and the two GE turbines were running at a hundred and ten percent power. The rotor blades were set as fine as they could go and still provide enough lift to keep them from slamming into the ground. At this speed, the turbine exhausts were providing most of his forward thrust and the stubwings most of their lift.

The Griffin was flying twenty-five miles an hour faster than the designers had ever intended her to fly. If Wolff kept the RPM governor on increase for too much longer, the turbines would be junk by the time he got back to their base, but the Wolfman really didn't care. Uncle Sam could always afford to buy a new turbine or two, but he was trying to save the government the cost of two funerals. Brass polish for the TPF honor guard was always real expensive.

"Lock on!" Mugabe suddenly yelled. "Lock on!"

Wolff instinctively slammed the cyclic over to the upper right side, stomped down on the right rudder pedal and pulled course pitch to the rotor blades. The speeding Griffin shuddered as the blades clawed the air again. The sudden torque increase threw the ship into a hard banked, skidding right turn.

Snapping the tail farther around to the right, Wolff dumped his pitch and the chopper flipped over onto her left side and fell like a stone. Suddenly, the Griffin was no longer in the air anywhere near where she had been just an instant before.

Wolff snapped his ship back upright and aimed it for a break in the fir trees. This low to the ground, he needed to put something between him and that Viper missile. A flash of light hit the right side of his peripheral vision. A Viper launch!

Kicking down on the left rudder pedal, he slammed the ship over on her side again as Mugabe triggered a salvo of decoy flares. The tips of the forty-foot rotor raised whirls of dead fir needles as it spun dangerously close to the ground. He was trapped. They were just too close to the ground to use the same evasive maneuvers that had gotten them away from the Viper before.

Wolff fought to bring the nose around, to get her through the break in the trees and he almost made it. The tips of the main rotor sliced through the tree branches as Mugabe frantically fired off another salvo of flares. The Griffin shuddered from the impact with the trees, but crashed through. One of the flares caught in a tree top behind them. The speeding Viper homed in on it and detonated.

Wolff was fighting the controls, desperately trying to gain airspeed again when the shock wave from the Viper's exploding warhead hit the ship. The blast slammed down hard on the Griffin, knocking it out of the air.

Turbines screaming, the Griffin hit the ground a glancing blow. The skids absorbed the shock and bounced the ship back up into the air. Wolff frantically fed full pitch to the spinning rotor blades, fighting to gain precious altitude. The blades touched a tree branch, threatening to pull them back down. The chopper lurched, but Wolff threw it into a left bank and they broke free above the tree tops.

They had escaped the Viper, but they were still not out of the woods. As low to the ground as they were, anyone with a slingshot could knock them down. But, for now, Wolff had to keep her skids kissing the tree tops until they reached the beach. He could risk taking ground fire, but if he got up high enough for another Viper to get a lock-on they'd be dead.

Within seconds, the Griffin flashed over the narrow, rocky beach and they were over the water again. With the turbines screaming on over-rev, Wolff kept the ship down on the wave tops frantically zigzagging while Mugabe salvoed his remaining flares one at a time. Five miles later, the pilot throttled back, pulled up and went into a wide banking turn to the west and Seattle.

As soon as he was at cruising altitude, Wolff relaxed, a big grin plastered on his face. "Well, we did it again, old buddy!"

Mugabe sat back in his seat and released the gun controls. "Shee-it!" he said, raising his face shield to wipe his face.

Back at the TPF Tactical Operations Center, Buzz Corcran watched as the Tac-Link data from Wolff's Griffin read out on the big screen in front of him. "There it is," he said grimly when the reading from the neutrino detector came up. "We've got that bastard now."

The captain turned to Lieutenant Avila. "How long till One Zero gets back here?"

Avila consulted his screen. "I've got their ETA as twenty-two minutes till touch down on the pad."

"I want to see them as soon as they get back."

"Yes sir."

Corcran walked back into his office and sat down

behind his desk. Now that they knew where the Trident warhead was, the ball was back in his court. He still didn't know what Dong planned to do with it, but if they could recover it before he moved it again, it wouldn't really matter. But that meant that they had to get their act together fast. Real fast.

Wolff's recon flight would have alerted Dong and Buzz had to put something together before the North Vietnamese had time to react.

He reached for the secure phone on his desk to report to the regional office that he had finally found the missing warhead. Denver was going to be real happy to hear the news and maybe he could get them to convince Washington to ask the Pentagon to lend him a hand with this problem. As far as Buzz was concerned, this was still a Tac Force operation, but he could sure use a little help from the armed forces to keep Dong's island isolated until he could mount his recovery operation.

In his cell in the depth of the prison, Tran listened intently to the faint voices of the guards at the end of the hall speaking rapidfire Vietnamese. Something had spooked them and his ears perked up when he caught the word, *phi co truc-thang*, Vietnamese for helicopter. If they were talking about choppers, he knew that it had to be a Griffin from Dragon Flight.

For the first time since he had walked into Dong's gambling hall, he felt that he just might get out of this mess. Someone had come looking for him. He realized, though, that they had actually come looking for the missing warhead. They probably had no idea that he was being held prisoner on the island.

But he also knew that it really didn't matter why they had checked the island out. If they had somehow detected the warhead, they would be coming to recover it

175

ASAP and, in the process, they would recover him as well. All he had to do now was to stay alive until the Tac Force arrived.

It sounded quite simple, but he was afraid that it might not be too easy to do. He had no idea what Dong had in mind for him, let alone why he had been left alive this long. And he knew that when the Tac Force hit this place, Dong would certainly have him and Baker killed immediately.

"Baker," Tran said sitting up in his bunk. "We need to talk."

"What about?"

"There's something going on that you need to know about. There may be a way for both of us to get out of this mess."

CHAPTER 22

Not only did Buzz have his full TPF staff assembled for the late afternoon planning session, but he had representatives from the Nuclear Weapons Commission, the Federal Prison System, the Navy and the Air Force in attendance as well. Everyone wanted to get in on the finale to this one. The Navy already had a small fleet in place effectively blockading the island and the Air Force was patrolling to keep all aircraft away as well.

"If everyone has been introduced," Buzz said. "I'd like to get started. First off, Mr. Jordan," he nodded to the federal warden. "I'd like you to give us a quick rundown on that prison site."

"Well, the Harrington Federal Confinement Facility was built in 1992 as a maximum security lockup to handle the overflow from McNeil Island. A few years after it opened, however, the island had to be evacuated because someone suddenly discovered that it was the nesting ground for some kind of damned bird on the endangered species list. I don't know what it was, sea gulls or something. The prison was abandoned at that time and has not been used since."

The warden flashed a map of the island on the screen. "As you can see, the main building is situated almost exactly in the center of the island. The building is five stories tall and is made of prefab concrete. The fenced in compound is outfitted by surveillance cameras.

"We have no idea if the security system has been made

operable again. But if Dong has got it working again, there's no way that your people are going to be able to sneak up on him."

"Is that an airfield?" Avila asked, pointing his light wand at what looked to be a short road leading to some large buildings on the corner of the screen.

"Yes, it is," the warden answered. "An all-weather, paved airstrip fifteen hundred feet long."

"Is it serviceable?"

The warden shrugged his shoulders. "I really don't have any idea, but it should be."

"How in the hell did Dong get access to that place anyway?" Buzz asked.

The warden shrugged. "We don't have any idea, we're just as surprised to find him there as you are. Under the provisions of the court order that made us evacuate the island, we can't even go back to check the place out once a year." He sounded disgusted. "Some bullshit about disturbing the nesting birds."

"So basically, no one has been in to inspect the place since 1994."

"That's about it."

"Can the Air Force provide us with satellite photos of the area?" Buzz asked.

"They've already been ordered," the Air Force officer answered, looking down at his watch. "You should have them in another hour or so."

"Good," Buzz said. He looked down to Jack Zumwald at the end of the table. "Now, how do you want to tackle this thing, Zoomie?"

Zumwald looked up from his notes. The Tac Platoon leader had been going over maps and photos all day and had come up with what he thought was a sound plan.

"Briefly, it looks to me like this guy's really got us over a barrel. Particularly with those Vipers. If we try a normal air assault, he's going to blow us out of the sky. It's the same story if we go for a parachute drop. It looks to be that we're going to have to go by sea, but that presents a problem as well.

"There's just not enough of us to hit the beaches like a John Wayne movie. We don't have any idea what Dong's forces are. We've used up quite a few of them in the last couple of days, but if he's got even fifteen to twenty men left, they could hold us up for days. Then, once we're on the island, we've got to storm that prison and that's going to be a real bitch.

"The way I see it, our only chance is to sneak onto the island, infiltrate as close to the prison as we can get and then let the Griffins blast a hole in the wall for us. Once inside, we can do our thing.

"One way we can infiltrate is to go in by submarine, but according to the maps I have, the water's too shallow to get in close enough. The other thing we can do is make a low altitude freedrop with our scuba gear a mile or so offshore and swim to the beach."

Zumwald stopped for a moment to take a sip of coffee.

"Personally," he continued. "I'm in favor of the freedrop and swim option. It leaves the operation totally under TPF control and we'll be working with our own people. The way I see it, we can load ten men into each of three choppers and make a wave top insertion. Then after they've let us off, they can stand off shore and wait for our call for fire support.

"Then we'll sneak up on the prison, call for the Griffins and have them blow a hole through both the fence and outer wall for us to make our assault."

"Do you have enough men?" Buzz asked.

"I think we can do it," Zumwald sounded confident. "From what we've seen so far, Dong's people really aren't that good. They've got some hotshot weapons, but they aren't that well-trained. With the Griffins backing us up, I think we can do it alone."

That was exactly what Buzz wanted to hear from his Tac Platoon leader. Calling in outside help at this stage of the game would only cause him headaches later on. If they could pull this off by themselves, it would take a lot of heat off the Tac Force.

"There's one more little thing that we've got to keep in mind here," Zumwald leaned forward in his chair. "That guy's supposedly got eight nuclear bombs on that island. Since by all accounts, he is not what you'd really call the world's most stable person, we've got to remember that when we storm that place, he might touch one of them off just for the sheer hell of it."

A stunned silence fell over the room. In the frenzy of planning, the cold reality of why they were planning the assault on the island in the first place had been easy to overlook. Zumwald's reminder put it back in the forefront of everyone's minds.

"And if he does," Zumwald continued, looking around at each man. "Uncle Sam is going to be in the market for a brand new Dragon Flight complete with Tactical Platoon and their glorious leader."

As soon as the command briefing in the TOC was over, Wolff called a meeting of all of the Dragon Flight chopper crews to go over their part of the plan in detail. If this thing was going to work, everyone was going to have to be on their toes with their heads up. If anyone got sloppy tomorrow, somebody was going to get hurt. Wolff's job was to see that that didn't happen.

"Okay, boys and girls," he announced when the flight crews had assembled. "Here's the bad news. We take off tomorrow at first light and assault Gray's Island. The good news is that due to the weather, we might be able to sneak up on the bad guys. But, then again, we might not."

"Gunner," Wolff called out.

"Yo!"

"You're C and C tomorrow."

Jennings sat bolt upright in his chair, a scowl on his face. He did not like that assignment at all, not even a little bit. If there was any chance of a fight, he wanted to be right in the middle of it. Flying the C and C ship, he would be well off to the side coordinating the air assault.

"Why me, Wolfman?" he shot back.

"Because Buzz wants it that way," Wolff lied.

"That sucks," Jennings said hotly. "I'm going to talk to Buzz about this."

"I wouldn't do that, Gunner," Wolff warned. "Not if you want to keep your gonads intact. He's not in what you'd call a real good mood right now."

Jennings sat back. He was thoroughly pissed off, but he knew better than to give Buzz a raft of crap about something like this when he had his back up.

"Okay," he sighed, sitting back in his chair. "I'll take the fucking C and C."

"Thought you would," Wolff grinned. "Avila will be running a full Air-Ground operation in conjunction with the Air Force on this one and you'll be tied in with him. They'll have ground attack F-18s on hand and F-15 Eagles flying high top cover. Our job, however, is to get in there and get the job done without having to call them in."

"If the Air Force starts popping caps on our mission," he explained, "The entire Tac Force is going to look like a bunch of assholes who have to call in their big brothers to bail them out."

"The hell with those flyboys!" someone said.

"My sentiments exactly," Wolff grinned. "Now back to the mission." He flipped on the holo projector and an aerial view of the prison sprang into life.

"Okay," he said. "Here's the drill. Zoomie and his boys are going in with us. We'll each take ten of them and

181

drop them off a mile or so from shore. Then we'll back off and try to hide till they call for us.

"Now, since we're going to punch a hole in the prison walls, the three attack ships will be carrying 2.75 inch armor-piercing rockets on their stubwing hard points. You'll have two seven round pods, fourteen rockets. Red is also mounting the 25 millimeters in the turrets, including," he looked at Gunner. "The C and C ship."

Jennings grinned. He was sure that he'd find a way to pop some caps tomorrow, C and C or no C and C.

"Once we go in, this is going to be a 'play it by ear' thing. I can't lay it out. We're going to have to stay flexible and respond to what Zoomie runs into.

"One last thing," Wolff's voice lost its usual playful note. "If you get a call to run, go for it. Don't even wait long enough to ask why. If you get the call, it means that Dong's about to pop one of his nukes.

"Also, if you see a bright flash of light, try to get away, don't wait for anything else. If you stay down flat on the deck and go balls out, you might be able to outrun the fireball."

"Are there any questions?" Wolff asked looking around the room. There were none.

"Okay," he said. "If that's all, I'll see you all on the flight line at zero six hundred hours."

The aircrew meeting broke up in a hurry as the pilots and gunners headed out to take care of last minute details. Now that the big mission was on, there was a lot to be done. Last minute checks of their choppers to be made, weapons to be cleaned, letters to be written, and most of all, getting a good night's sleep.

Wolff stopped Mugabe in the hall outside the conference room. "Go on ahead without me," he told his co-pilot. "There's something I've got to take care of. I don't know how long I'll be, so don't wait up for me."

"No sweat, partner," Mugabe answered. "Just don't be

late tomorrow morning."

"I'll be there," Wolff promised.

The pilot hurried out into the wet night and spotted Legs walking toward their quarters. "Yo! Legs!" he called out. "Wait up."

Sandra stopped and turned around. When Wolff got up to her, she finally said something that had been on her mind for a long time. "Rick, will you do me a favor and please quit using that stupid nickname. For Christ's sake, everybody's got legs."

Wolff was stunned, he had never known that she was sensitive about her Dragon Flight nickname. "Sure Flight Officer Revell," he said.

"What do you want?" she asked.

"Since I kept you past the dinner hour, I thought the least I could do is buy you something to eat."

"And a few drinks afterward?" she asked, her good humor immediately evaporating.

Wolff held his hands up in a disarming gesture. "Whoa, lady," he said. "No way. I don't make that much more in my paycheck than you do. If you want to get drunk, you can damned well pay for it yourself."

"Cheap bastard," Sandra laughed. "Okay, you're on. Where do you want to go?"

"Dressed like this?" he looked down at his well-lived-in dark blue flight suit. "How about the club?"

"Let's do it."

CHAPTER 23

The Coast Guard Officers Club

Everyone at the Officers Club bar looked up when Wolff and Sandra walked past on their way to the dining room. Several inviting glances were offered, but she totally ignored them this time. She wasn't interested in fancy uniforms worn by bright, eager, young faces right now. Tonight she wanted to talk to someone who spoke her own personal language, a cop and a pilot.

The waitress showed them to a table in the dining room and took their orders for two sirloin steak specials, both blood rare, with salads. The two chopper cops talked shop until the food came and then they both dove right into it. It had been a long day for both of them.

"That was good," Sandra said putting her napkin on the table and leaning back in her chair. She fixed her eyes on her dinner companion. "Okay, now what's this all about?"

"What do you mean?" Wolff frowned.

"You haven't tried to make a pass at me all evening."

"Me? Make a pass at a cop?" the pilot protested. "You think I'm crazy?"

Sandra laughed. "Come on Rick, I've been through this drill with you more than once. I know your little routine by heart and you're just not your usual smart assed self tonight. So, what's up?"

Wolff got a very serious look on his face. It was all too easy to forget that a first class mind lived inside that gorgeous body. He knew better than to underestimate Sandra Revell, but sometimes even he forgot for a moment and let his gonads do his thinking for him. It was time to get his act back together.

"Well," he started slowly. "I wanted to talk to you about the mission tomorrow." He stopped and seemed to struggle to find the right words.

"What do you mean?"

"Well," he started again, "considering what you've been through the last couple of days, I wondered if maybe you'd like to stand down on this one." He shrugged. "Maybe work with Avila in the ops center. Something like that."

Sandra stared at him for a long moment and carefully composed her thoughts. "Rick," she said quietly. "I know that you're Dragon One Zero, the Griffin flight leader. You're a good cop and an even better pilot. I know that you do your best to take care of the rest of us, both in the air and on the ground."

She paused and took a deep breath. "But if you try to keep me off the flight line tomorrow morning, I'm going to Buzz and request an immediate transfer out of here. After, that is, I have kicked your ass up between your ears."

Sandra's voice had been low, controlled and as soft as velvet. But Wolff felt the steel under the velvet and knew that he was treading on dangerous ground.

Had it been one of his men that he was concerned about, he would have simply dropped him from the mission and left it at that. With Sandra, however, he knew how hard she worked at her job and he had a lot of respect for her. He was only trying to make this easier for her. But damn him, all he was doing was completely lousing it up.

"Look," he said. "I . . ."

"No! You look, *sir*," she shot back. "You and I go back a long time. We've been in a lot of deep shit together and I owe you for a couple."

Sandra paused when she remembered the time that Wolff had flown off her wing over the Pacific, guiding her back to land after her pilot had been killed. They had been intercepting a shipload of drugs, but the ship had been armed with anti-aircraft machineguns. The same burst of fire that had killed the pilot had knocked out most of the flight controls, making it almost impossible to keep the Griffin in the air. But all the way back, Wolff had flown alongside her, talking her through it, coaching her with all the tricks of the trade that he had learned from his years in the air. Little things that had never been printed in any flight manual, but that kept her from crashing into the ocean. She certainly owed him for that one and a couple more as well. But regardless, she was not going to put up with any of this.

"But," she went on. "If you try to pull me off this mission because you're trying to protect me, I'm going to stomp your young ass flat."

"No," Wolff protested, "That's not it at all."

"Then you think I've lost my guts."

Wolff sat back and sighed. "Not at all. I was just trying to give you a break."

Sandra abruptly stood up. "When I want a break, Wolf-man," she said quietly, "I'll ask for it myself. You copy?"

Wolff nodded. "Loud and clear."

Spinning around, Sandra walked out of the dining room. Wolff slowly shook his head; now he had really loused things up. Damn it anyway, why did women have to be so damned touchy.

Sandra Revell was still under tight control when she walked past the bar on her way out of the club. The look on her face and her body language kept any of the assembled Coast Guardsmen or cops from saying a single word to her. And that was probably a good thing; the way she was feeling she would probably have torn the first guy who said anything limb from limb.

The wind was in her face when she stepped outside. She stopped for a moment and lifted her head and let the fine mist cool her face. The cold felt good. A second later, she continued on her way, but she didn't know where she was going. Her footsteps automatically led her down to the flight line where the Griffins sat side by side on the tarmac.

She slowly walked up to her ship, the new Dragon One Four. It looked exactly like the old one, except that it was intact. It wasn't broken and burning on a rooftop with her trapped inside the cockpit. She shuddered and lifted her face to the rain again to wash the memory away.

She was just turning to go when a figure suddenly stepped out from the shadows behind the next ship in line. She started and stepped back.

"What are you doing out here so late, Legs?" Red asked before he saw the look on her face. When he did, he put his tool box down and hurried over to her. "Is there something wrong?" he asked.

Sandra shook her head. "No Red, I'm fine."

The maintenance chief reached out to take her arm. "Come on into my office. I've got a pot of coffee on and you sure look like you could use a cup."

Red was the only man in the Tac Force who could have gotten away with putting his hands on her tonight, but she let him guide her into the maintenance office.

Red's office was its usual mess. Grease smudged work orders and maintenance updates littered his desk. Cigar butts overflowed from two ashtrays, one on each side of the desk. For a man who was so meticulous about his work, he lived like an animal and a sloppy animal at that.

With a sweep of his hand, he cleared a spot in the middle of the desk top for her. "Here," he said, pulling out the chair. "Have a seat."

187

Usually Revell didn't like men to pull chairs out for her, but there was something so innocent and old fashioned about the way Red did it that she didn't mind. She sat down and tried to compose herself while Red poured coffee in a cup that had last been clean when it first left the factory. "How do you take yours?" he asked.

"Barefoot," she answered.

"That's good 'cause I'm all out of fixings."

He handed her the coffee and reached for his own dirty cup. "I've got all the ships purring like kittens," he said. "There won't be any problems with them tomorrow."

Now that he had Revell in his office, Red didn't know what to say to her. Even though his only love was helicopters and no one in the Tac Force had ever heard him say a single thing about a woman, Red was not unaffected by Sandra Revell. In his case, however, she made the usually gruff and outspoken maintenance chief shy and tongue tied.

"When we installed the 25mm turret on your new bird," he continued, looking away from her. "We found a short in the firing circuit that took us most of the afternoon to track down. But don't worry, we got it fixed. You won't have any problems with it. That's going to be a good ship for you, I guarantee it."

Sandra took a careful sip from her coffee cup. The rumors were right, Red's coffee should be reported to the Environmental Protection Agency as a Class One hazardous chemical, but it was hot. She suddenly felt chilled and welcomed the warmth.

"Man, you sure had a scare the other night, didn't you?" Red asked. He knew that he was running off at the mouth, but he couldn't seem to stop. "We listened to it on the radio and we were sure that you and Gunner were going to get killed."

Sandra shuddered. She had been thinking exactly the same thing, but somehow, it made it even more terrifying to hear it from someone else.

"I really have a lot of admiration for you guys," Red went on. "I know it can be a real bitch up there sometimes. A few years ago it didn't seem to be so bad. But now, what with all the weapons the bad guys have, it takes a lot of guts to go up there everyday and do what you guys do.

"Back in the 'Nam it was pretty bad. But, at least there we had all sorts of back up. You know, air support, artillery, things like that. And we didn't have to worry about killing some civilian by mistake. If some dumb ass farmer got in the road of a gunship, that was just too bad, we wasted him and no one worried about it."

Sandra suddenly realized that this was another thing that had been bothering her. She had read the after-action report about the downing of her ship and learned that the kid who had fired the rocket at them had only been sixteen years old. He should have been at home doing his schoolwork, not shooting at police helicopters.

Revell wasn't a rookie cop trying to answer the great questions of life after putting down her first armed suspect. She had killed before in the line of duty and normally it didn't bother her. If a suspect was armed and threatening, it was her sworn duty as a police officer to neutralize him, or her, and to do it fast.

This time, though, the standard rationale for killing in the line of duty wasn't working for her. Even though she had not pulled the trigger on that kid herself, she felt a wrongness about his death. She also knew that just because he had only been sixteen, did not mean that he was automatically innocent. She knew full well that an armed teenager was often far more dangerous than an armed adult. Somehow, though, it seemed tragic.

Red shook his head. "Man, I wouldn't have your job for nothing."

Sandra almost agreed with him. Regardless of what she

had told Wolff tonight, she wasn't too sure that she wanted to keep on being a hotshot chopper cop. She'd wait till she got back from the mission tomorrow, however, before she pursued that line of thinking any further.

She quickly drained the last of the coffee and got to her feet. "Thanks Red," she said. "I really needed that."

"No sweat. Anytime."

Red watched her open the door and start back down the rain-slickened tarmac to the barracks. That was one tough lady. He hoped that whatever it was that was bothering her didn't get in the way tomorrow. It was going to be tough enough for her without having something cluttering up her mind.

After Revell left, Wolff didn't even stop off at the bar for a drink. He didn't feel like listening to those assholes swapping stories. He too walked out in the rain, but he headed for the main gate and a long solitary walk to clear his head.

Showing his TPF ID card to the gate guard, he headed out on the street toward downtown Seattle. He turned the collar of his flight jacket up around his neck and stuck his hands deep in his pockets.

Maybe Sandra was right and he had overreacted. Maybe he was being overprotective, but maybe there was a reason for it though. He knew that he would not have had a talk like that with any of the other Dragon Flight personnel, but none of them affected him like she did.

For all his smartmouth, Wolff had been careful to keep his private life separate from Dragon Flight. Sure, he drank and chased women with Mojo, but that was different. He and Mugabe were friends. He had been careful to keep his distance from most of the other cops, particularly the female cops. He knew better than to mix the potentially explosive situation of a sexual relationship with

190

the job. Fishing in the secretarial pool was not without its dangers.

Nonetheless, his bantering with Sandra had a serious side to it. And he wasn't too sure what he would do if she ever did take him up on one of his propositions. As a cop, he knew better than to ever take her to bed. But, as a man, he knew that he if he ever did get her into bed, he would never want her to leave.

Wolff put in two miles along the road before he turned around. Problems or not, he had to get some sack time if he was to look and feel his very best tomorrow. After all, it wasn't everyday that he went up against a maniac with an island full of nukes.

When he finally got back to his room in the Coast Guard BOQ, he found his roommate sound asleep. Whatever the mission, that was one thing he could always count on. Mojo was not about to let anything interfere with his sack time.

Wolff quietly got undressed and set his alarm. He tried hard not to think about the mission, or about his run-in with Sandra. It was funny, but for all the time that he had known her, he had never known that she didn't like her nickname.

CHAPTER 24

The Coast Guard Base

Mugabe was down on the flight line right as dawn broke. The day was overcast and the visibility was only about a thousand meters, but it was not raining. Yet. He glanced down at his watch; if the weather held, they'd be in good shape.

Wolff was late again this morning, but that was not unusual at all, the Wolfman would probably be late for his own funeral. Mugabe was always the first to suit up and get down to the flight line before every mission. This was a practice he had started doing back in the good old days when he had first flown for the CIA, the DEA and anyone else who would give him a mercenary's paycheck to man the weapons from the left seat of a gunship.

Being alone at dawn with the hulking, silent war machines always calmed him before a mission. It was his form of meditation, to stand and drink in the silence, knowing that it would soon be gone. In just a few minutes, the flight line would be full of the chatter of nervous voices, the clanging of steel on steel as weapons were loaded, and the whine of the starter motors as the chopper turbines were fired up.

For now however, the co-pilot was alone with his thoughts. Thoughts of his missions in the past and of the flight they were to make today. This was going to be a real motherfucker today, there was no doubt in his mind about that. But when he really thought about it, they had all been gold plated motherfuckers. There was no such

192

thing as an easy mission when someone was shooting at you. It was only when a mission was over, and he could look back on it, that he could put it into its proper perspective.

He knew that if this one didn't go tits up in a big way, he would be able to look back some day and tell light-hearted war stories about the assault on Gray's Island. Someday, though, but not this morning.

He looked across the wet tarmac and saw his pilot round the corner of the maintenance building headed for the flight line. As usual, he was still getting dressed as he walked, pulling on his gloves and zipping his flight suit.

"At least we've got good weather for it," Mugabe said when Wolff walked up.

The pilot glanced up at the overcast. "Yeah. We're going to need all the help we can get if we're going to sneak up on those bastards."

Wolff sounded annoyed and Mugabe was puzzled at his tone of voice. Usually the pilot was excited before a mission, but today Mugabe knew that something was weighing on his mind. "You okay?" he asked.

"I'm fine," Wolff answered curtly, looking around to see if anyone else had shown up yet. "Where the hell is everybody?"

"Lighten up, man, they'll get here."

While Wolff paced impatiently, the rest of Dragon Flight slowly assembled in twos and threes and stood by their choppers. Gunner and Legs were the last to arrive and Mugabe noticed that Wolff did not greet Sandra or give her any of his usual wise ass comments. In fact, they seemed to be avoiding one another.

Then it hit him, maybe she had been the business he had had to take care of last night. If his hunch was right, it didn't look like the meeting had not gone well at all. Jesus! This was all they needed today, some kind of beef going on between those two.

"Okay," Wolff called out as soon as everyone was present. "Let's get this show on the road."

The pilot started his walk-around inspection of his Griffin at the front. The bug-eyed sensor turret on the extreme nose broke the sleek lines of the ship, but gave the machine a menacing, "don't mess with me" look. He checked the sensor heads and then knelt on the damp tarmac to examine the belly turret.

The barrel of the newly mounted 25mm Chain gun stuck out two feet farther than the lighter 7.62mm gun that was usually fitted in the turret. He reached out and ran his hand over the cold, wet steel for reassurance. "This'll help even up the odds," he said grimly.

Reaching under the ship's belly, he popped open the latches to the ammo storage bays and looked inside. Just like the doctor ordered, two thousand rounds of 25mm high explosive and armor-piercing ammunition for the Chain gun lay in the portside ammo bay. A thousand rounds of 40mm for the grenade launcher was in the other. He snapped the hatches back in place, locked them and stood up.

"What's the matter," Red growled from behind him. "Don't you two flyboys trust me to do my job?"

"Just about as much as you trust me to do mine," Wolff snapped as he turned around.

Red took the unlit cigar out of his mouth and looked at the young pilot. What in the hell was wrong with everyone this morning? He knew that this was going to be a tough mission, but this was not the first time that Dragon Flight had stepped into some deep shit. He didn't see it as a reason for everyone to be wound up this tight.

The maintenance chief shrugged and walked away shaking his head. This whole place was crazy today.

Next, Wolff checked the two 2.75 inch rocket pods hanging under the stubwings. Although the Griffin had been designed primarily for police work, it still had four military style hard points under the stubwings that could accommodate military type ordnance. Anything from rocket pods to drop tanks or five hundred pound bombs could be carried if the mission required their use.

Today the three assault ships were armed with seven round rocket pods loaded with shaped-charge, anti-tank rockets. A salvo of them would bust a hole in any concrete wall in any prison in the world. They weren't as good for use against ground targets, standard HE warheads would have been much better. But today the main job was to open a hole in the prison walls so Zoomie and his team could go to work. And that required the armor-piercing capability of the shaped-charge warheads.

Wolff checked to see that the firing wires were secure and then moved on to check the fuel filler doors and the battery compartment. A quick check of the sharply swept, shark like, tail fin and shrouded rotor completed the walk-around.

The pilot glanced down at his watch, it was time. "Mount up," he called out.

The four crews climbed into their respective machines, strapped themselves and started their cockpit checklists. Ten men split off from Zoomie's formation on the edge of the runway and climbed into the back of each of the ships. This time, they carried lightweight underwater breathing apparatus as well as their normal weapons.

Wolff looked over his shoulder as the men climbed into the back of his ship. "Where's Zoomie?" the pilot asked.

"He's flying with Browning and Tac One," one of the Tac Team said.

As soon as the pilots called in to report that their pre-flights were done, Wolff keyed his throat mike and radioed the TOC. "Dragon Control, this is One Zero, we're go."

"Dragon Control, I copy," Mom answered. "Stand by."

"One Zero copy."

Now came the hard part, waiting to take off. Even on a

195

good day, waiting was something that Wolff had never been good at and today it was driving him up a wall. He wanted to get this thing over and done with one way or the other.

Finally the word came from the TOC for them to start up.

"Dragon Flight," Wolff said, hitting his mike switch. "This is One Zero, crank 'em."

The whine of four starter motors echoed off the side of the hangar as the Griffin pilots hit their start switches. The turbines fired up with a roar and the hot smell of burning kerosene shot through the cool morning air as the rotors started turning.

As soon as the engine checks were made, Wolff gave the word. "This is One Zero, follow me."

Overloaded as they were with the men of the Tac Platoon, Wolff led the Griffins out onto the runway in a line formation. One at a time, the choppers started off, their tails high in a gunship take off. Halfway down the tarmac, their airspeed came up and they lifted off. Forming up over the base, Wolff led Dragon Flight up to five thousand feet and banked to the west and their appointment at Gray's Island.

As soon as the four choppers cleared the shipping in Seattle's harbor, Wolff led the Griffins back down to wave top level for the approach to the island.

"You'd better keep a sharp eye out, Mojo," the pilot warned. "If there are any fishing boats out here, at this speed we'll run right into them before we can spot them in this shit."

Mugabe was already watching his radar readouts. "I'm watching for 'em, Wolfman. You just fly this damned thing, okay?"

Wolff didn't bother to answer him. Obviously, he wasn't the only one who was a little testy today.

* * *

Five miles away from the island, Jennings banked away from the rest of the formation and went into a low orbit. As C and C ship for the operation, his job was to coordinate the attack and he would not make the approach with the choppers carrying the assault units.

With his skids kissing the wave tops, Wolff led the three assault ships in closer. In the passenger compartments of the Griffins, Zoomie's men had already donned their lightweight scuba gear and face masks. Their weapons and tactical helmets were in waterproof cases strapped on their backs. Special swim fins fitted over their combat boots so they could hit the beach running.

When he was a little more than a mile off shore, Wolff slowed down to just a few miles an hour, flying parallel to the beach. "This is it," he called back. "Hit it!"

The Tac Team leader slid the side doors back and one by one, the Tac cops made the few foot drop into the water below. In seconds, they were out of sight under the water, forming up to make the swim to the beach.

As soon as all of the Tac Platoon were in the water, Wolff banked away leading the three assault ships back to their holding position where they would wait for Zumwald's call.

Though the water was cold, the swim went quickly and twenty minutes later, the assault units reached the beach. Like sea lions coming ashore, the Tac Teams wiggled up to the surf line, dropping their breathing gear in the water and struggling to get out of their wet suit tops.

Lying half in the water, they quickly unlimbered their weapons cases and donned their helmets. Once communications were established, Zumwald ordered Tac Team Three to move forward and take up covering positions at the top of the beach.

Zumwald had picked a spot to land where the trees were closest to the water's edge. But from where he lay in the water, he saw that the sea breeze was rapidly dissipating the morning fog. The dark, camouflaged shapes of the men crawling up from the surf line were clearly visible against the sand. If Dong had anyone waiting for them, they were going to be in a world of hurt.

Jack Zumwald had always wanted to fight an all-out war and this morning he finally got his chance. Tac Team Three didn't get a hundred meters from the beach before all hell opened up on them from the woodline. Under a hail of automatic weapons fire, the men of Tac Three ran for cover behind the rocks and bushes. The men waiting in the surf backed down deeper into the water.

"Dragon Leader," Zumwald called. "This is Command Two, we are pinned down on the beach. We're taking heavy fire from the tree line and need help ASAP. How copy?"

"Two, this is Dragon Lead," Wolff answered, throwing his machine into a hard bank. "Good copy. We're on our way, keep your heads down."

"Dragon Flight, this is One Zero," Wolff radioed the other two ships flying with him. "Zoomie's pinned down on the beach. Turn the wick up and follow me. Fire on anyone or anything not wearing Tac Force cammies."

The three Griffins spread out in a vee formation with Wolff's One Zero at the point. Mugabe dialed in HE grenades for the 40mm, flicked the Chain gun off safety, wrapped his fingers around the firing controls and watched the range numbers flicker past at the bottom of his sight picture. Eight hundred meters out and ten meters off the wave tops, he triggered his 25mm.

The Griffin's airframe shuddered as the heavy cannon opened up. The other two ships followed Mugabe's lead and the woodline erupted in a storm of fire.

When the choppers opened fire, Zumwald got to his feet. "Let's go!" he yelled, leading the charge. If he was ever going to get his people off the beach, this was the time to do it. Also, he was freezing to death lying in the water.

He need not have hurried, however, the three man outpost Dong had positioned to watch over that part of the beach was wiped out on the first pass by the gunships. Torn, mangled bodies was all he found when they reached the woodline.

There was a radio by one of the bodies, however, and the microphone lay at the end of its cord as if the man had been making a call right as he was blown apart.

Zumwald keyed his throat mike. "Dragon Lead, this is Tac Two, they had a radio. Get ready for a party."

CHAPTER 25

Gray's Island

Now that the element of surprise had been lost, Wolff decided to head on inland to look for targets of opportunity. "Dragon Control," he called to the C and C ship. "This is One Zero. I'm going in to take a look around, One Two and One Three will stay with Tac One and you might as well move in closer too. How copy?"

"This is One Four," Jennings radioed back. "Good copy, we'll be there in zero two."

Wolff grinned behind his face mask. He had heard the elation in Gunner's voice. Even burdened with the C and C duties, if he was over the island, he might be able to get in a few shots after all.

Wolff kept down low and detoured far around the prison building. Even though the outpost had probably warned their leader that he was being attacked, there was no point in being too obvious about it.

"We're full defensive," Mugabe announced, flicking on the mirror skin and the IRCM module. In the heat of battle, the gunner had not forgotten that their opponents were well armed. He leaned over his sensor readouts, scanning the entire spectrum for any sign of trouble.

"Heads up!" Mugabe warned. "I've got aircraft on the ground at the air strip."

"What are they?"

"They look like civilian light planes, but there's a biz jet down there and at least one chopper. Wait! I've got movement on the jet. It's trying to take off!"

"One Four," Wolff radioed Jennings. "This is One Zero, we've got customers on the air strip and they could be transporting the bombs. One of them's a bizjet preparing to take off. I'm going after him, you keep the others on the ground." The Tac Force was under Rules of Engagement Charlie again and any airplanes on the island were assumed to belong to the bad guys.

"One Four, copy," Gunner called back. He switched his radio over to the emergency frequency that all aircraft monitor. "All aircraft on Gray's Island, this is the Federal Tactical Police. Shut down your engines immediately or be fired upon."

The minute Jennings started transmitting, pandemonium broke out on the airstrip, pilots and crew ran for their planes and frantically started their engines. The small jet sitting at the end of the runway, a blue and white, twin engine Lear Jet executive ship, released its brakes and started down the runway.

"The bizjet's rolling," Mugabe said.

"I've got him." Wolff hauled back on his cyclic control to pull the ship up into a climb to gain precious altitude. Speed and position were success in any aerial combat and since the jet was so much faster than his Griffin, the only way that he could catch up with it was if he dived down upon it from above.

But this was also where things got a little sticky. The higher he flew, the better target he was for getting a Viper up the tail pipe. He was hoping that with the aircraft trying to take to the sky, Dong's men wouldn't fire and risk hitting one of their own planes by mistake.

The Griffin had gained fifteen hundred feet and was heading out to sea by the time the jet hit rotation speed and tucked up her landing gear to make a run for it. Wolff hit the over-rev switch on the governor and pushed his nose over in a dive. The chopper quickly accelerated past her maximum design airspeed and rapidly closed with the fleeing jet.

The Lear Jet hugged the waves, desperately trying to gain enough speed to outrun the diving Griffin, but it was too little, too late.

"Don't let him get away, Mojo!"

"Not to worry," the gunner answered as he opened up on the small plane from a thousand meters out. He was aiming for the tail mounted engines to force it down, but air-to-air gunnery is not a precise thing.

The 25mm cannon shells tore through the tail section and walked their way on up to the wing root. Two hits and the wing folded back against the fuselage. The Lear slowly rolled over and plummeted into the sea.

"Mayday! Mayday!" Wolff radioed on the Air-Sea Rescue frequency. "This is Tac Force Dragon One Zero. I have a Lear Jet crashing at sea two miles to the southwest of Gray's Island. Send Air Sea Rescue ASAP."

Back over the air strip, Jennings and Legs were doing a good job of keeping everyone else on the ground. The helicopter had tried to escape, but a quick burst of 25mm had sent it crashing to earth. The rest of the pilots abandoned their planes and were standing on the runway with their hands held high in the air.

"Gunner," Wolff radioed. "We don't have time to babysit those people right now. Get them away from those planes and then put a round in each aircraft to disable it."

"Sitting ducks, my favorite target," Jennings radioed back.

Now that no one was going anywhere, Wolff flew back to see how Zumwald's assault force was doing.

Zumwald's assault forces had worked their way up to the edge of the clearing bordering the prison compound. Resistance in the woods had been light and scattered. The Griffins hovering overhead had been able to keep the Tac

202

Teams out of trouble. But the Tac Platoon leader was under no illusions about what kind of a fight Dong's men were going to put up from the prison building itself. It was a fortress and gave the Boa Hoa all the advantages. Even now, a heavy machine gun on the roof was making it dangerous for the Tac cops to break cover.

The Boa Hoa had everything going for them where they were, thick concrete walls, good firing positions and cleared open ground that the cops would have to traverse to get to them. The only thing they didn't have were gunships on their side and that alone might be what would make the difference.

It was time to call on the Griffins to even up this fight a little. "Dragon Lead," he radioed. "This is Tac One. I could use a little help getting the door opened."

"This is Dragon Lead, copy, I have the locksmiths on the way."

In seconds, Wolff's One Zero appeared accompanied by One Three, one of the other rocket laden gunships. "Where do you want it?" Wolff radioed.

"How about right in the middle of the ground floor?"

"Coming up."

While One Three walked its cannon fire across the rooftop and took out the machinegun, Wolff swooped down and lined up on the middle of the wall. Flames shot from the front of rocket pods as Mugabe triggered his first salvo. Trailing plumes of dirty white smoke, four 2.75 inch rockets lanced out from under the Griffin's stub wings, streaked for the dull concrete wall and hit simultaneously.

The ground floor erupted in a flash. Black smoke and gray concrete dust shrouded the wall. Mugabe's second salvo of four rockets impacted in the center of the smoke. Broken chunks of concrete flew up into the air as the wall went down.

When the dust cleared enough to see that a breach had been made in the wall, Zumwald brought his hand forward. "Come on boys!" he yelled. "Let's get it!"

Screaming their battle cries, the ten man lead assault team leaped to their feet and charged after their leader. Off to the side, the other Tac Team poured fire into the break in the wall.

Zoomie was the first man to charge through the shattered wall. The exploding rockets and support fire had taken care of anyone who might have wanted to argue with him. He found himself in a large room with a corridor leading off to the side. He took cover behind a large chunk of concrete and ordered the other team inside.

Once they were safely inside, Zumwald signaled his men to fan out and follow him down the hallway.

Even deep in his prison cell, Tran could hear the gunfire outside. It sounded like war had broken out on the island. He sat up and slipped his shoes and jacket on. He wanted to be ready on the off chance that an opportunity to escape might present itself.

Baker roused himself from the other bunk. "What's going on?" he asked.

"The cavalry's arrived."

"What?"

"I think the Tac Force is here," Tran smiled. "And we just might get out of this after all."

The cell door clanged open and two of the Boa Hoa walked in. "The colonel wants you," one of them told Tran.

"What about me?" Baker squeaked.

The guards ignored the technician as they slipped a restraint over Tran's wrists. Baker leaped to his feet. "You can't leave me here!"

One of the guards savagely slammed the butt of his weapon into the technician's belly. Baker folded up and fell back on the bunk. The two guards led Tran out and locked the cell behind them.

The guards took Tran to a control room where Dong was seated behind a brightly lit panel that held several TV monitors. The Boa Hoa leader was dressed in the same camouflage uniform and red beret as his men wore. A stolen U.S. Army M-25 assault rifle was slung over his shoulder.

"Your Chopper Cops have disrupted my plans," the gang leader said, pointing to a scene on one of the monitors, showing a Griffin hovering over the wreckage of several light planes. "They are closing in on me. But they are going to suffer the same fate as their fathers did when they invaded my country, they are falling into a trap. My key men and I will be long gone before they get here."

"It's not too late to stop this," Tran said.

"It is for me." Dong reached out and flipped a switch on the control panel. Blinking lights came on and numbers appeared on a digital readout. One of the bombs is being left here," Dong explained, pointing to the control panel. "And it is controlled by this. As soon as my men and I are clear of the island, this bomb will be the first one to detonate."

Tran was stunned. The nightmare was really going to happen. "If you do this, Dong, you'll be tracked to the ends of the earth. You'll be found and killed no matter where you try to hide."

"That is a chance I will gladly take," the gang leader said. "History will never forget this day!"

Tran shook his head slowly. "You're out of your fucking mind."

Dong's face hardened. "Take him back to his cell," he ordered in Vietnamese.

The guards took Tran's arms and led him away. On the way back to his cell, a sharp explosion shook the building. Both guards looked around in panic, losing their grip on Tran's arms for an instant.

The cop lashed out with his foot, catching one of the

guards on the outside of his knee. The man screamed and fell to the floor, his leg at an awkward angle. The other Boa Hoa spun around to meet Tran's bound fists right under his ear. He too fell to the floor.

The first guard was reaching for his fallen weapon when Tran kicked him again, this time in the throat. The Vietnamese gagged and clawed at his throat, tying to force air through a crushed larynx.

Tran ignored him as he reached down for the combat knife from the second guard's boot top. Drawing the blade with both hands, he stabbed deep into the man's heart. He withdrew the knife and turned back to the first guard, but he had already strangled to death.

Now he had to find a way to use the knife to cut through the plastic restraints holding his hands together. That, however, proved to be more difficult than killing the guards had been. He was finally able to brace the point of the blade against the wall and saw his wrists against the edge to sever his bonds.

Rubbing his wrists, he reached down and recovered one of the guard's AK-94s and an extra magazine. His heart pounding, Tran slowly made his way down the corridor toward the sound of the explosions, the AK held at the ready. All he had to do now was to keep himself from being killed when Zoomie's boys stormed in and spotted him.

This was the first time that being Vietnamese had been a real disadvantage in his line of work. The Tac Teams were going to see his Oriental face and open up, thinking that he was one of the Boa Hoa.

CHAPTER 26

Gray's Island

After Zumwald's men disappeared into the prison building, Wolff ordered One Three to stay in position over the prison in case they needed an assist. He then turned his machine around and left to look for targets of opportunity. So far, this operation hadn't been all that bad, at least from the Griffin's standpoint. The Tac Platoon had taken a few lumps. But it seemed like whatever the mission, the guys on the ground always got stuck with the heavy end of the stick.

He made a run over the air strip, saw that Jennings had the situation well under control and started back for the prison.

"Wolfman! Down there!" Mugabe shouted.

The pilot glanced down and saw a dead black helicopter lifting off from a camouflaged position behind the prison. It was an unfamiliar design, twin turbines, five blade rotor, stub wings, fixed landing gear and a stepped canopy. The chopper banked and he saw that it was carrying a nose turret and weapon pods under the stub wings.

"That's a gunship!" he yelled. "I think it's Red Chinese, a Havoc!"

As a gunship pilot himself, Wolff kept track of the other armed choppers in use throughout the world. He vaguely remembered reading that Red China had stolen one of the Russian's latest military helicopters, an Mi-28 Havoc, and were making copies of them. At least this ship looked like the photos he had seen of the Russian Havoc. And if it was, things were going to get interesting real fast.

"Wolfman," Mugabe shouted. "This guy's not showing up on my targeting radar!"

"What the hell is he, some kind of stealth chopper?"

"Beats the shit outta me, man, but I've got to go optical if we're going to take him out."

"Do it!" Wolff ordered as he threw his ship into an interception course for the mysterious black machine.

Since his boyhood days, Wolff always dreamed of flying fighters. He had read every book about aerial combat that he could get his hands on and had built dozens of models of his favorite fighter planes. Simulated dog fights with other old warbirds were fun, but it was not the real thing. Today, it looked like he might finally get his chance to do it for real.

The Havoc quickly accelerated and headed right for the airstrip where One Four was orbiting. "Heads up, Gunner," Wolff radioed. "You've got company."

Jennings was flying in a low slow orbit and, at Wolff's call, he frantically tried to get out of the way of the gunship rapidly closing with him. He took the easy way out and ran for a clear space in the trees as the Havoc opened up with its cannon.

Wolff took a deep breath and racked One Zero around to face the Havoc right as the big helicopter started its firing run on Gunner.

If he turned the wick up all the way on over-rev, he could make almost two hundred and fifty miles an hour. He had the 25mm Chain gun and the 40mm grenade launcher in the chin turret to fight with. The Mi-28 Havoc, if he remembered right, could do almost three hundred miles an hour and was armed with air-to-air rockets and a machine cannon, probably the same deadly 23mm multi-barrel weapon that armed the Russian MiG-29 Fulcrum jet fighter.

The odds weren't too bad. The Havoc was faster, but

Wolff was sure that the Griffin was more maneuverable. The only advantage the black machine had were the air-to-air missiles she was packing on the ends of her stub wings.

When the Havoc missed Jennings's chopper, it went into a wide banking turn, gaining altitude to come back to try it again.

"Mojo," Wolff called over the intercom. "Keep that bastard off Gunner!"

A half a mile away, the enemy gunship completed his turn and started back for the air strip. This time, though, it found Wolff in its path and lined up for a head-on shot at the newcomer. Wolff twisted his throttle back to cut his RPMs and hauled up on the collective to change the pitch of his rotor blades for maximum maneuverability. It was time to dance.

With a kick at the rudder pedals and a savage pull on the cyclic stick, the Griffin suddenly wasn't where she had been in the sky anymore. She had jumped off to the right and was hanging almost motionless in the air, her tail high.

Glowing bright orange, the Havoc's 23mm cannon tracers flashed through the spot the Griffin had occupied just a moment before.

Wolff snapped the tail around as the Red Chinese machine flashed past them. Mugabe gave it a short squirt from the Chain gun as it passed.

"Lead him, Mojo!" Wolff yelled over the intercom when he saw the 25mm tracers fall far behind the speeding gunship. "Lead the bastard!"

The Griffin's firing controls and gunsight were designed to shoot at ground targets, not something moving at a closing rate of five hundred miles an hour. By jet fighter combat standards, this was not fast at all, F-15s and MiG-29s closed at well over two thousand miles an hour. But it was two or three times as fast as anything that a helicopter gunner usually had to deal with.

It was impossible to feed in enough lead through the sights to hit something moving that fast. He was going to have to do some bare eyeball shooting to get a hit. He'd let Wolff get closer next time and wait until the last possible moment before firing.

"You okay?" Wolff called over to his gunner.

"Yeah," Mugabe answered back, taking a deep breath. "I can't lead that fucker, Wolfman, he's going too fast. I can't keep the sights on him."

"I know. You're going to have to use a little Kentucky windage while I try to stay out of that bastard's road. Heads up! Here he comes!"

This time the Havoc didn't make a gun run on them. The enemy pilot circled around them like Indians circling a wagon train in a western movie, just looking for a place to strike.

Wolff turned his gunship with the Red Chinese machine, keeping him in clear sight in front of him. Suddenly, the Havoc climbed straight up, high into the sky above them.

"Watch him, Rick!"

"I got him."

The enemy gunship dropped down on top of them like a diving hawk. He had figured out their weak spot, an attack from above.

Wolff whipped the tail of his machine around and twisted his throttle to max RPM as he pulled the nose up in a climb to meet the diving Havoc. He was trapped. If he tried to run now, he was dead. With the Havoc above him, any direction that he tried to turn, the enemy chopper could easily turn with him, bring his cannon to bear and blow him out of the sky.

All he could do now was to meet him face to face and shoot it out.

The Havoc started firing short bursts from his cannon, jinking his turret from side to side as he fired, spreading the pattern of the shells.

Rick saw the flicker of fire from under the gunship's nose, but there was little he could do about it. He could only try to snake his chopper around in the sky to present as difficult a target as possible.

If he tried to turn or dive away, he'd be cold meat.

Suddenly, he saw flame spout from the tips of the Havoc's stub wings. He had fired his air-to-air missiles!

In the gunner's seat, Mugabe had also seen the launch, his gloved finger stabbed at the decoy flare launcher, firing flares from both sides of the ship. As soon as the flare were away, he got back on the firing controls of his weapons, centered the diving enemy machine in his helmet gunsight and opened up on him.

The Red Chinese gunship suddenly banked off to its right to avoid Mugabe's burst of fire and the missiles flashed past harmlessly on either side of the Griffin. Whether the decoy flares had lured them away or the forced maneuver had broken the guidance from the Havoc, didn't matter. The missiles missed and now it was their turn.

Wolff threw his machine over onto her side in a hard banked left turn. Halfway through the turn, he slammed the cyclic over to the other side, rolling the Griffin over onto her right side. A sharp kick down on the right pedal brought her tail around and he was in a firing position right behind and off to the side of the enemy machine as it passed.

The Havoc pilot saw Wolff's maneuver and knew that he had to shake the Griffin off his tail. Twisting the throttles to his twin turbines past their stops into over-rev, he pulled in maximum pitch and put the nose into a steep dive. The heavy Havoc pulled away from the smaller Griffin like a falling rock.

"Jesus Christ," Wolff said in total disbelief. "Look at that son-of-a-bitch go!" He glanced down at his own airspeed

211

indicator and saw that it was reading almost two hundred and fifty miles an hour. There was no way that he could catch up with the fleeing enemy machine. "He must be doing two hundred and seventy five."

Wolff followed into a dive as the Havoc pilot put his ship down on the wave tops. The flat black of the Havoc's camouflage paint blended in with the water and made it difficult for Wolff to spot him until he saw the sun glint off his spinning rotors.

Suddenly, the enemy gunship pulled into a sharp skidding right turn. Using the brutal torque of the five massive rotor blades to spin him around, the Havoc completed a hundred and eighty degree turn faster then any chopper Wolff had ever seen.

This time, the Havoc bore straight on in, firing as he came. This time it was Wolff's turn to give way. He broke to the right again. But this time, the enemy pilot followed, turning with him as he continued firing. Big glowing orange balls of the 23 millimeter tracer rounds flashed past Wolff's canopy.

Wolff's instinct was to try to dive away from the fire, but he knew that would be a fatal mistake. He had seen that the heavier enemy gunship could easily outrun him in a dive. His only hope now was in his Griffin's greater maneuverability.

In the heat of the fight, Wolff had completely forgotten about Jennings and Legs. Gunner had followed the twisting, turning dogfight out over the water and now he saw an opportunity to lend a hand.

As the Havoc pilot concentrated on following Wolff's wildly twisting Griffin, Gunner closed in for a firing run. Sandra was having the same problem Mugabe had had trying to target the Havoc. Her radar and IR sensors didn't show the ship either and she too had to use her optical sights.

She didn't get any hits, but her attack made the enemy

pilot break off his run on Wolff. "Thanks, Legs," Wolff radioed as he savagely hauled his ship around to follow the Havoc. "I've got him now."

Wolff's flight path brought him in on an angle to the rear of the black Havoc, a deflection shot. "Get 'em, Mojo," he yelled to his gunner.

Mugabe knew that an aerial deflection shot was the hardest one in the world to make and he didn't have a compensating gunsight to compute the proper firing angle. But, it was the only shot he had, so he took it.

Again the 25mm Chain gun roared, shaking the airframe, but his first burst fell to the rear of the speeding enemy machine.

"Lead him!" Wolff yelled.

Mugabe fed in two leads to his sight picture and fired again. This time, he saw his rounds hit in the rear of the enemy machine. One round brought a puff of black smoke from the starboard turbine pod. He fired again, but the enemy ship was no longer in his sights.

The Havoc pilot had stomped down on his rudder pedal, feathered his rotor blades to minimum pitch and hauled back on his cyclic, all at the same time. The Red Chinese put her nose up and skidded sideways, losing speed as fast as if he had opened a dive brake.

The maneuver caught Wolff completely by surprise. His speeding Griffin flew right on past the Havoc and into the path of its guns again.

The enemy pilot was just pressing the cannon trigger when he saw a flash of light in the sky above him and glanced up. Jennings's Griffin was diving on him, its turret ablaze as Revell held down the Chain gun's trigger.

The barrage of 25mm high explosive shells tore the black helicopter apart in midair. A second later, it exploded in a fireball that slowly fell to the sea below.

Gunner flew up alongside Wolff's Griffin. "You okay?" he radioed.

Wolff waved back. "Yeah, thanks."

Zumwald and his men were steadily working their way through the ground floor of the prison. The Boa Hoa were resisting, but they were no match for his well-trained tactical cops. Meter by meter, the Tac Force cleared the halls and corridors. They took no prisoners.

Tac Team One huddled behind a counter in front of the prison infirmary when one of the men saw movement down the hall. He pitched out a grenade and followed it up with a long burst from his MP-5.

"Cease fire, Goddamnit," Tran yelled from down the hall. "I'm Lieutenant Tran from the field office."

"Hold your fire!" Zumwald called out to his men. "Come on out with your hands up!" he ordered.

Tran staggered out into the open, his hands high up over his head.

"Lieutenant Tran?" Zumwald asked, taking in the slight figure in rumpled civilian clothes.

"Yes, I'm Tran. Quick, give me your radio, man. I have to warn the choppers."

"Warn them?"

"Yes, damnit!" Tran almost yelled. "There's a nuke in here and it's set to go off in a few minutes."

CHAPTER 27

Gray's Island

As soon as Tran got through to the TPF TOC with his message about Dong's booby-trapped nuke, Buzz ordered Zumwald to break off his attack and get the hell out of there ASAP. Dragon Flight was ordered to pick the assault force up and get out of the area immediately.

"I guess we'd better get going, then," Zumwald said.

"Not so fast," Tran answered. "I think I know a way to get this thing stopped."

"What!"

"Yeah, the guy who rigged that bomb is in a cell in the basement," he explained. "He fixed it and now he can damn well unfix it."

Zumwald shook his head. All he wanted to do was to get the hell out of here, not screw around with a booby-trapped atomic bomb. "Let's go talk to him," he sighed.

Baker was hiding in the corner of the cell when the two cops showed up. "Stand back while we blow the door," Tran said.

One of Zumwald's grenades took care of the lock and Tran pushed the shattered door open. "It's all over, you can come out now."

"Can I go home now?" Baker pleaded.

"There's one little item that you've got to take care of first," Tran said. He quickly told Baker what Dong had told him and the technician grew pale.

"I didn't think he'd do that," Baker said.

"Well, he did and now you're going to take care of it,"

215

Tran said. "Where is it?"

"Probably in the room I worked in."

"Take us there quickly."

The bomb was unimpressive, just a white cylinder a meter and a half long and half a meter in diameter. It was hard to believe that so much destructive power could be contained in such a small package. On one end of the bomb was fixed a small box. A window showed seconds ticking off.

"How do we turn it off?" Tran asked.

"You don't," Baker answered. "It has a non-reversible circuit. You interrupt the electronic current in any way and it automatically goes into nuclear detonation."

"So there's no way to prevent it from going off then?"

Baker shook his head. "No, it's easy to stop," he said. "All you have to do is to blōw it up with high explosives."

"You're crazy!" Zumwald exploded. "No fucking way am I going to let you . . ."

"No, really," Baker broke in with an explanation. "If you knock the fissionable material out of alignment, it won't detonate."

"Jesus!" Zumwald said. "Will it work?"

"It's the only chance you have to stop it."

Zumwald shook his head. "What do we use for explosives?"

"There's a room full of C-4 demolition blocks right down the hall."

Outside the prison, the Griffins were setting down one at a time in the clearing beside the fence. Zumwald's men ran from the main gate and scrambled on board the choppers. As soon as one ship was filled, it lifted off and, keeping low to the ground, sped away as fast as its rotors blades could carry it.

Wolff was the next to land, leaving Jennings still in orbit

overhead. "Where's Zoomie?" Wolff asked the cops clamoring into the back of his machine.

"He stayed in there," one of them answered, pointing back at the prison. "He and the officer from the field office found that bomb and they're trying to disarm it."

"Oh shit!" Wolff switched to the command frequency and keyed his mike. "Command One, this is Dragon Lead."

"Command One," came Buzz's voice in his headset. "Go ahead."

"One Zero, we have another little problem here. We're loading out, but Tac One and Lieutenant Tran are still inside the building trying to disarm that bomb. I'm going to wait for them, how copy?"

"Dragon One Zero, this is Command One," Buzz was almost shouting into the radio. "Negative. You are to leave the island immediately. Do you copy?"

"This is One Zero, that's a negative, we still have men on the ground."

"Clear the island, One Zero, that's an order! Do you copy?"

Wolff didn't even bother to answer. He switched over to the ship-to-ship frequency and ordered Jennings to land so he could transfer his passengers to his ship. As soon as One Four lifted off with the last of the assault force, Wolff switched to Zumwald's frequency. "Tac One, this is One Zero, come in."

"Tac One, go."

"As soon as you're through playing with your toy, I'm ready to haul your asses out of here."

"You'd better get clear while you still can, Wolfman. If we screw up, this place is going to be a big radioactive hole in the ground."

"I've never been in the middle of a nuclear fireball," Wolff radioed back. "It might be fun."

"You're out of your fucking mind!"

"I've heard that somewhere before, but I'll be waiting for you."

"Thanks, buddy."

Zumwald placed the last of the blocks of C-4 explosive around the bomb casing and Baker quickly wired it to the rest of the explosives. "How are we going to set this thing off?" the Tac officer asked.

"You're not," Baker answered.

"What do you mean?"

"You and the lieutenant are going to get out of here," the technician answered glancing at the flashing lights on the digital readout on the control box. "You've got six minutes before I pull the pin on this grenade fuse. Five seconds later, the C-4 will go off. The explosion should break the bomb up and prevent it from going into a nuclear detonation sequence. If it works, you'll be safe. If it doesn't, well," he paused. "You'd better be as far away from here as you can get."

"Are you sure about this?" Tran asked.

"Yeah," Baker answered. "I'm sure. It could be the one worthwhile thing I've done. Now, get the hell out of here, will you."

Tran and Zumwald didn't waste time arguing with the man. If that was the way he wanted it, it was all right with them. They spun around and dashed for the stairs. The two men ran our of the main gate of the prison, sprinting for Wolff's Griffin sitting on the ground just outside the fence with its rotors spinning.

Wolff pulled pitch as they scrambled into the back of the chopper. "It's going to blow any second!" Zumwald yelled up to the pilot. "Get the hell out of here!"

Wolff twisted the throttle all the way against the stop, hit the over-rev switch to the turbine governor and hauled up on the collective, pulling maximum pitch on the rotor. The

Griffin leaped into the air like a gut-shot rabbit, her rotor blades clawing the air.

Deep inside the prison, Baker watched the seconds click off. He wanted to give the chopper all the time he could to get away, but he also didn't want to be too late.

The clock clicked over to fifty seconds and he pulled the pin on the grenade fuse. He didn't even try to run for cover. If for some reason, the fuse malfunctioned, he had another grenade fuse ready and needed to be there to try it again.

Wolff kept the Griffin flat on the deck with her turbines howling. His airspeed was up over two hundred and sixty-five miles an hour thanks to a strong tail wind. In the back, Zumwald was counting off the seconds. ". . . three, two, one, zero!"

There was no flash of blinding white light and no crushing shock wave hammered them into the water.

"Well, I'll be Goddamned," Zoomie said softly. "It worked!"

As soon as Dragon One Zero's skids settled on the tarmac, at the Coast Guard Base, Tran slid the side door open and jumped out running for the TOC. He had to get the search organized for the one nuke that Dong had time to put in place.

While the Griffins quickly refueled, Zumwald's men drew a fresh ammunition load and climbed back on board. In minutes, they took to the air again in case there was something that they could do to aid the search.

Tran had that situation well under control, however. He quickly learned that only two local military bases had any connection with Vietnamese businesses that might have been directed by the Boa Hoa, the Bremerton ship yards and McCord Air Force Base. Tran made a gut decision and concentrated on McCord.

At the Air Force base, the Air Police frantically searched for the nuke. The entire base and surrounding area had been evacuated and a team from the Nuclear Weapons Commission accompanied the search teams as they tore into every nook and cranny. Once the bomb was found, their disposal men would attempt to disarm it.

The blue painted foot locker that had been delivered by the roach coach was found within the first hour.

The EOD man studied the black box grafted onto the end of the nuke. "It's not too bad," he said. "Whoever did this knew what he was doing."

"He should have," the Air Police officer said. "He was trained by the Navy."

"I should be able to deactivate this thing in just a few minutes."

"What's the chances that you can do it without setting it off?"

"Oh, I'd say a little better than average," the technician grinned. "The nice thing about nukes is that if you make a mistake you never know it."

The officer shuddered, but he knew the EOD man was right. He focused the camcorder to continue taping the attempt to deactivate the weapon and transmitting the picture simultaneously. This way, if the EOD man fucked up and made a mistake there would be a record of what he had done wrong and the next man to work on one of Dong's bombs would know how not to make that same mistake.

"Captain!" Ruby yelled. "They disarmed the nuke!"

Buzz sat back in his chair. Thank God, now they could finally wrap this monkey fuck up and go home. "Tell Zoomie and Wolff that they can stand down now."

"Yes, sir."

When Wolff brought his Griffin in for a landing, he saw

that Sandra was waiting for him off to the side of the taxi ramp. He shut the turbines down and climbed out of the cockpit as she approached him. She had taken off her helmet and was fluffing her blond hair as she walked.

Wolff waited till she got closer. "Thanks for the save out there," he said sincerely.

She stopped and looked straight at him. "Not too bad for a cop who lost her guts, was it?"

"Sandra," Wolff began. "Look. I'm sorry . . ."

"You owe me a dinner for that one, Wolfman," she said. "And this time you can buy my drinks too."

Before Wolff could reply, she had walked past him. The pilot shook his head as he watched her walk off. Women.

"Wolff," he heard Buzz's voice behind him.

The pilot turned around to face his commander. "It's over, isn't it, Captain?" he asked.

"Just about," Buzz answered. "The Navy still has to recover the nukes from those two planes you guys trashed and initial reports confirm that Dong was aboard that Havoc."

Wolff nodded. "But our part of it's done."

"Yes, it is," Buzz agreed. "Now we get to go back to Denver for a week's maintenance and re-outfitting before we go back on alert status."

"Don't we get any time off for good behavior?" Wolff grinned.

"You're lucky that I don't send you and Mojo to fly sea gull patrol in Bumfuck, Alabama like Red keeps asking me to do," Buzz said. "That little number you pulled deserves at least that."

"It worked, didn't it?" Wolff grinned.

"It's a damned good thing too," Buzz shot back. "That's the only reason that you're not facing a disciplinary board action when we get back."

"Well, it was just one of those judgment calls," the pilot shrugged. "You know how it is, Captain."

Buzz stood silent for a moment fighting back a smile. Yes, he did know how it was. There had been a time when he would have done exactly the same thing that Wolff had done. He had not been a chairbound commander long enough to have forgotten that the man on the ground, or in the air in this case, looks at a situation differently than the man does sitting safely behind the radio miles away. Had he been there, he knew that he would have stayed on the ground too, orders or not.

"Yeah," Buzz said. "At least until next time, hotshot."

WARBOTS by G. Harry Stine

#5 OPERATION HIGH DRAGON   (17-159, $3.95)
Civilization is under attack! A "virus program" has been injected into America's polar-orbit military satellites by an unknown enemy. The only motive can be the preparation for attack against the free world. The source of "infection" is traced to a barren, storm-swept rock-pile in the southern Indian Ocean. Now, it is up to the forces of freedom to search out and destroy the enemy. With the aid of their robot infantry—the Warbots—the Washington Greys mount Operation High Dragon in a climactic battle for the future of the free world.

#6 THE LOST BATTALION   (17-205, $3.95)
Major Curt Carson has his orders to lead his Warbot-equipped Washington Greys in a search-and-destroy mission in the mountain jungles of Borneo. The enemy: a strongly entrenched army of Shiite Muslim guerrillas who have captured the Second Tactical Battalion, threatening them with slaughter. As allies, the Washington Greys have enlisted the Grey Lotus Battalion, a mixed-breed horde of Japanese jungle fighters. Together with their newfound allies, the small band must face swarming hordes of fanatical Shiite guerrillas in a battle that will decide the fate of Southeast Asia and the security of the free world.

#7 OPERATION IRON FIST   (17-253, $3.95)
Russia's centuries-old ambition to conquer lands along its southern border erupts in a savage show of force that pits a horde of Soviet-backed Turkish guerrillas against the freedom-loving Kurds in their homeland high in the Caucasus Mountains. At stake: the rich oil fields of the Middle East. Facing certain annihilation, the valiant Kurds turn to the robot infantry of Major Curt Carson's "Ghost Forces" for help. But the brutal Turks far outnumber Carson's desperately embattled Washington Greys, and on the blood-stained slopes of historic Mount Ararat, the high-tech warriors of tomorrow must face their most awesome challenge yet!

Available wherever paperbacks are sold, or order direct from the Publisher. Send cover price plus 50¢ per copy for mailing and handling to Pinnacle Books, Dept.17-353, 475 Park Avenue South, New York, N.Y. 10016. Residents of New York, New Jersey and Pennsylvania must include sales tax. DO NOT SEND CASH.

MYSTIC REBEL by Ryder Syvertsen

MYSTIC REBEL (17-104, $3.95)

It was duty that first brought CIA operative Bart Lasker to the mysterious frozen mountains of Tibet. But a deeper obligation made him remain behind, disobeying orders to wage a personal war against the brutal Red Chinese oppressors.

MYSTIC REBEL II (17-079, $3.95)

Conscience first committed CIA agent Bart Lasker to Tibet's fight for deliverance from the brutal yoke of Red Chinese oppression. But a strange and terrible power bound the unsuspecting American to the mysterious kingdom— freeing the Western avenger from the chains of mortality, transforming him from mere human to the MYSTIC REBEL!

MYSTIC REBEL III (17-141, $3.95)

At the bidding of the Dalai Lama, the Mystic Rebel must return to his abandoned homeland to defend a newborn child. The infant's life-spark is crucial to the survival of the ancient mountain people—but forces of evil have vowed that the child shall die at birth.

MYSTIC REBEL IV (17-232, $3.95)

Nothing short of death at the hands of his most dreaded enemies—the Bonpo magicians, worshippers of the Dark One—will keep the legendary warrior from his chosen destiny—a life or death struggle in the labyrinthine depths of the Temple of the Monkey God, where the ultimate fate of a doomed world hangs in the balance!

Available wherever paperbacks are sold, or order direct from the Publisher. Send cover price plus 50¢ per copy for mailing and handling to Pinnacle Books, Dept.17-353, 475 Park Avenue South, New York, N.Y. 10016. Residents of New York, New Jersey and Pennsylvania must include sales tax. DO NOT SEND CASH.